TOM HENIGHAN

TOURISTS FROM ALGOL

Stories Of The Unexpected

THE GOLDEN DOG PRESS, Ottawa, Canada

Canadian Cataloguing in Publication Data

Henighan, Tom
        Tourists from Algol

I.   Title.

PS8565.E582T6 1983   C813' .54   C84-090004-X
PR9199.3.H45T6 1983

Ontario Arts Council
20th anniversary
1963-1983

© The Golden Dog Press, 1983

ISBN:978-0-919614-46-8

The Golden Dog Press gratefully acknowledges the assistance accorded to its publishing programme by the Ontario Arts Council and The Canada Council.

Printed and bound in Canada.

Dedication: To Marilyn

"What interests me is not the laws, but the exceptions to the laws"

Julio Cortázar

Acknowledgments: *Anthos, Antigonish Review, The Apalachee Quarterly, Phoebe: The George Mason Review, The Canadian Literary Magazine;* Chez-FM, Ottawa.

Contents

The Explorers

O n the last expedition, just before the end of the world, they
set out to find the Yeti.
The Yeti had been known to most of them for a long
time, but of course none of them had ever actually seen it. Each had
been acquainted with someone who made that claim, but all they
could put together between them were seventeen footprints, a black
shape bounding across the snow one hundred yards distant, and a
collection of dubious old bones.

Their leader, Lord Hutton, a ruddy-faced man of great strength
who remembered Thesiger, invited them to his estate in Northum-
berland to talk it over. Foucault, the philosopher and Alpine
climber, couldn't come; he had fallen over a tree stump in his yard
and had sprained his ankle. His apology arrived in a telegram just
as Evans left Manchester, bringing with him some photographs he
had been sent from Nepal only a few months before. Sir Harry
Groves was in London picking up his fees as a bit player in the new
epic, *Film Without Humour*, which several directors had agreed to
collaborate on. This movie was supposedly to explore the nature of
the serious, though a few contended (supported by Sir Harry in
casual conversation) that the serious had no nature; it was simply
the condition of being without humour, which explained why it was
such a difficult mode to sustain. Sir Harry arrived first, eager for
news.

"What the devil is Colin up to?" was the way Chuck Legg put it
to himself when he got Hutton's letter at his ranch house outside of
Taos, New Mexico. Like the rest of them he was rather old, seventy-
seven to be exact, and the transatlantic routes, even supposing he
had been close to them, were very dangerous during this period of
phony war just before the final send-up.

"I'm for it," was what he said when he finished the letter.

The drawing room at Peak House was lovely. Originally by Adam, it had been salvaged and reassembled by Lord Hutton's grandfather when the northeast coast of England had drifted away in a storm one winter. Actually, the old boy had been after the Durham Cathedral door knocker, but the room was a find nonetheless, and it had been worked in around the existing fireplace, roaring now with a kindly ancient warmth as it was.

The first thing they looked at were the Evans photographs. Some of them had tears in their eyes as they saw the blank white nothingness of snow.

"South col of Kanchenjunga," Sir Harry was not slow to affirm.

"Bloody impressive shot," Lord Hutton added.

"Looks like footprints in the foreground, for sure," suggested Legg, who had made it over on Pan Am.

"Wait until you see the closeups," Evans concluded, delighted at this response.

For the non-aficionado should be added a world of description, for how many, other than CIA spies, Russian chemical warfare experts, Chicom infiltrators, and TV Eyewitness News cameramen have trekked those forbidden spaces?

To be brief — *the colossal mountain mass soared up to a giddy height — to the ethereal workshops in which the eternal snow spins the delicate webs which it sends down the slopes of the mountain as offerings to the sun, where the winds gambol at their will, and where the stillness of death divides sovereignty with the bitter cold.*

The next photograph (actually a colour slide) showed clearly some mighty strange looking footprints.

The footprints could have been made by a Yeti. The group looked on in silence; these were experienced explorers — they refused to jump to conclusions, but they were profoundly moved, and over the cognac later, and after several more pictures, a council of war was held.

It was then and there agreed to launch a new expedition. Conditions were far from ideal, as Lord Hutton was not slow to point out. The world was trembling on the verge. Travel was becoming increasingly difficult and expensive. Government assistance was out of the question.

Lord Hutton stood a few feet from the fire, his weathered old face made into a grotesque mask by the flickering light. Hands clenched into fists, he surveyed his comrades with slightly squinting affection.

"Well, lads, are we for it?"

2

The answer was evident in each man's hearty affirmation.

During the next few days, orders went out in many directions, to Fortnum and Mason, Abercrombie and Fitch, Black's, White's, Green's, Bhicajee Cowasjee, and to sundry other surprised suppliers in the more elegant districts of London, New York and Delhi.

The orders came back with all speed. They made up the usual freight of such adventures: ropes, skis, boots, pitons, the Bible and various kinds of expensive cameras. Nothing was wrapped in brown paper. The oxygen masks were the latest, the Sherpas the oldest, to be contracted on the spot.

At the first base of Katmandu, the three Englishmen and the American waited for Foucault, who had promised to join them but did not. Assuming that he was a casualty of the accelerating violence, they made their plans without him. Their guess was not entirely wrong. Forced into an unaccustomed idleness by his sprained ankle, Foucault had become aware that his young wife was being unfaithful to him, and that in fact she had been deceiving him for years. Greatly disturbed, but exercising splendid self-control, he fell back upon his philosophy of tragic acceptance learned from Nietzsche, to which he added the idea drawn from Freud through Lacan that the concrete had to be taken precisely for what it was: the concrete. He regretted of course that in the case of his wife his perceptions of the real had led him astray, and he also lamented this interruption in his pursuit of the Yeti, which he had hoped to study as a species of linguistic exotica, without any metaphysical preconceptions. Nonetheless, he proceeded to Paris to complete the purchase of supplies and to give a paper on "The Self-Sufficiency of the Now" at the nine thousand seven hundred and twenty-fifth meeting of the European Psychoanalytic Association, only to be caught directly in the first major exchange of nuclear rockets between the Americans and the Russians. Strolling near the Jardins du Luxembourg he heard the sinister alarms and watched the skyline of the city erupt in the splendour of a dazzling pink white halo of fire.

"Revolution!" he cried out, shaking his fist at this telltale apocalypse of oppression, and refusing to run for the Metro. He was struck down where he stood by an enormous wave of heat which his senses translated under shock into a wild breath blown straight off the mountains on the coldest Himalayan heights.

Katmandu was far removed from the terrible accidents of the period of nuclear confrontation. While a temporary peace ensued and negotiations went furiously forward in the world capitals (apologies being made for the mistake that killed several millions) the

3

explorers, virtually self-sufficient, decided to cross over into Tibet in order to begin their search. At Sangsang, in sight of the venerable Brahmaputra, they recruited porters and prepared to work back into the Himalayan chain, following the caravan routes and riverbeds and moving upward steadily into the great glacial highlands which they already knew from many years past.

Foucault's presumed death was a sad burden to them in the early stages of the trip, but under the influence of the awesome landscape, even such a sharp loss must fall into place. They set out through bright April weather, following the cold glitter of a nameless stream toward the cloudless peaks. Fold after fold of low hills coiled before them, dark flexed flanks of the mighty massif. A few villages of sprawling huts housed them en route, or they camped under the steep shelter of cliffs, watching the sky for signs of a change in the weather. Struggling across a giant spur of the central ranges they felt themselves hauled up by encircling arms. It was as if they stood still while the mountains slowly engulfed them. In time that was no time they found themselves skirting bright glaciers that seemed poised and tilted forever under a wedge of sky.

In the middle of the third week, a storm drove down upon them from the heights as they prepared to camp. Darkness came on quickly but the snow whirled about them, polished to sinister brilliance by the angled last light. Hurriedly, they urged the ponies in toward the rim of a sheltering valley. The storm broke over the valley, a careless fury of edges cutting and tearing at their half-anchored haven. They crouched under improvised shelters as the night passed wearily.

At noon of the next day the storm abated, but there was trouble with the porters. Four of them refused to go further, claiming that their dreams had collectively predicted disaster for the expedition. Lord Hutton, questioning them closely, could learn nothing more. It was decided that Chuck Legg would accompany them to the nearest village and attempt to recruit replacements there.

As he was preparing to leave, the weather brightened, and Legg unpacked his treasured pearl-handled revolvers from the baggage and strapped them under his weatherproofs. The pistols, which he had acquired while he was adviser to one of the Oman oil sheiks, were a kind of good luck charm. All the while he had worn them he had made vast sums of money which enabled him to buy several thousand acres in the vicinity of Lobo Mountain, New Mexico. There he had established various enterprises as his tastes changed: an experimental sexual recreation center, a library of books by and

4

about Immanuel Velikovsky and a farm and factory to produce goat's milk cheese. Lean and rugged, his reflexes quick as ever despite his years, Legg followed the four mounted ex-porters whose names happened to be Barkha, Tokchen, Shamstang, and Sersok down the dim trail that stretched away through many yawning valleys to the town of Kampak. On the way he practiced several Tibetan dialects, discussing the afterlife and attempting to translate sentences from *Alice in Wonderland*, which the porters took to be a sacred text. After three days they reached the village but, alas, no replacements were to be found there. Disappointed, Legg said goodbye to the four and started back. On the second day, halfway up a steep mountain climb, he came upon a surprising sight: a tent made of black yak's hair, its anchoring thongs singing and creaking in the rather stiff wind. Inside was a nomad and his wife eating a dinner of nettle spinach. Politely they welcome him and offered him a bowl of tasty barley beer. The effect of this brew was stronger than the explorer had remembered. After a while the woman's dark eyes seemed to glitter with a faint mocking light. She offered to read his palm and told him he would never find the Yeti. But he had not mentioned the Yeti to them; or had he? The effects of the beer made it difficult to remember.

The next day the man invited him to go hunting. Legg was anxious to test out his revolvers. Riding out, they saw only some wild sheep vanishing over a distant rocky ridge. Legg fired a few shots, but they were out of range. The report crashed and echoed over the mountain. The Tibetan was delighted, his round wrinkled face eager, he hauled out his own weapon, a clumsy antique muzzle loader, and let out a blast that seemed to shout back at them from all the ravines. Legg rocked in his saddle, surprised and amused at the weapon. He asked if he might examine it, and was just sitting down to do so when he heard a sudden faint roaring from far above. A vague intuition suggested to him what it was. He shouted to the Tibetan, jumped into his own saddle and galloped off as fast as the pony would take him. The Tibetan did not move. Legg stopped for a moment and cried out; he was trying to warn the fellow, shouting and pointing. The Tibetan did not move. In despair Legg reached for one of his revolvers and fired quickly into the air, stirring up the sluggish pony and making him run. In a few precious seconds he had got the pony trotting at a good speed. The poor beast seemed terrified. Legg leaned down over the animal's neck and stole a look back at the Tibetan, who was staring at him in astonishment, not moving at all. The poor fool, Legg was thinking, the poor fool. It was one of his last thoughts that trip out. The crazed pony found its footwork useless in mid-air: stumbling out of stride, it had pitched forward across the edge of a thousand foot crevasse, taking its astounded rider with it.

The next morning, sunrise was spectacular. Waking up in their tent the Tibetan and his wife were inclined to ascribe the display to their strange guest, whom the hunter had seen with his own eyes fly off into the region of the eternal spirits.

The explorers waited two weeks for the missing Legg, sending out two of the remaining porters in search of him, only to find that neither news nor even the porters returned. A series of sunrises and sunsets of spectacular coloration led them to believe that another nuclear holocaust was possibly in progress, and, saddened though they were by the disappearance of their friend, they determined to push on. Now that civilization as they had known it was ending, they might as well continue their quest.

In another week, during which there were no more portents in the sky, they reached the Valley of Katchanga with their five remaining porters and made the first significant discovery of the expedition.

While digging up some snow to be boiled for water, Yengla, one of the porters, discovered a large and mysterious footprint etched in the hardpack at the protected base of a large boulder. Wild with excitement, the three explorers crowded round.

"Not human," Evans asserted, peering down at it.

"Not animal either," Hutton assured them, scrambling over with one of the cameras.

"Gentlemen," Groves solemnly announced, "we've discovered the eighteenth known footprint of the Yeti." He went to work at once taking measurements, casts and endless photographs.

They were sure there must be more prints, but after three days and a thorough search of the area for miles around, they had found nothing. It was difficult not to be disappointed. Regretfully, they agreed they must split up. Groves insisted on staying to continue the search for footprints in the many caves at the other end of the valley. Yengla would remain with him, while the other four porters would go with Hutton and Evans.

When the others had taken leave Groves moved his camp to the largest of the caves, a narrow black slash in the snow-encrusted side of the valley. Inside, the cave was more spacious, stretching back into a ribbed gloom of branching archways. With the help of Yengla Groves built a low wall of loose stones across the mouth of the cave as a windbreak and they gathered brushwood for the cooking fire and set their belongings in order. The next day the exploration of the caves began, starting with the one in which they had camped. They traced two passages to impenetrable fissures in the remote recesses of the rock, marked out trails and returned. The third passage was more interesting, because it branched into two further ones, and one of these into two further ones. At the end of a week a whole series of caves had been marked out for further investigation. It was then that the extraordinary pink sunrises and sunsets began again. Yengla, who had heard the explorers talk about the end of the world, insisted on taking a week off to go to the nearest village from where he hoped to get a message to his family. Groves continued the exploration of the caves on his own.

Groves swung his burly frame through cavern after cavern, twirling his splendid old-fashioned mustache and reciting lines from all the various films he had played bit parts in as he mugged shamelessly to the nonexistent cameras. From time to time he mouthed passages from Tibullus or Horace or put on his cassette recording of the Aeneid delivered in Latin by himself, and the close and fetid air boomed with the sonorous ancient melodies of Aeneas' descent into Avernus. Groves had gone from classics at Cambridge to films at Ealing, returning at intervals to his Norfolk birthplace where he had stored his splendid collection of first editions of the works of his ancestor, H. Rider Haggard. His dreams of making the ultimate film version of *She* had been interrupted by the general economic decline and the urgent call of Lord Hutton to his final attempt to locate the elusive Yeti. Alas, now he feared, and rightly, that the project would disappear into the limbo of unrealized wishes. Nonetheless, as he sat back with his pipe every evening around the fire, he worked meticulously over the script, building the lost city of Kôr out of the thousand separate scenes he had so painstakingly imagined from the original.

It was a few days after the departure of Yengla that he made his discovery. Groves was re-thinking the cave scene in *She* in which Billali shows Horace Holly the relic of the women's foot. He was wondering whether he should insert a flashback to convey the burning of the woman's corpse, or rely on Billali's narrative, and his mind was so full of vivid pictures rapidly shuffled that he at first missed the second extraordinary track at the mouth of the deep left-branching cave which he had so far barely explored.

It was a footprint that leapt to life in the beam of the torch, one that he had missed on his earlier foray because it was imprinted on a

7

small ledge or shelf of stone. He stared down at it now, stopped in his tracks, his breath coming fast with excitement. Another single mysterious footprint, larger than a man's, belonging to no known species of ape or bear, a footprint stamped not on the bare rock but on the softer more recently mudcaked surface of the stone. The nineteenth known footprint of the Yeti, here in this very cave!

The next few hours were spent in furious and meticulous recording of the evidence. Photographs in colour and black and white, another cast, the taking of some samples for laboratory analysis — when all this was finally done, Groves collapsed in fitful and exhausted sleep, determined that on the next day he would penetrate the left-branching system of caves in search of further clues.

After breakfast and a walk through the valley to take the air, with one last look at the sinister pink of the dawn, Groves began his descent into the deeper recesses of the mountain.

Loaded down with knapsack and ropes, reflecting metallic markers, camera, tape-recorder, and even a special gun equipped with a hypodermic needle, Groves penetrated farther and farther into the caves. Wearing a miner's headlamp and a light strapped to his belt, he edged along grim corridors of stone not seen previously, perhaps, by any human eyes. Alas, no camera crew followed, no network distribution, and only his own voice-over, moment by moment, burst forth in a curse or a song. Gone were the endless spaces of Himalyan grandeur, gone were the peaks and the shining glaciers; he had succeeded in burying himself in a single tiny crack of those great ranges.

Time passed, progress was slow — it was difficult to make a thorough search along every inch of passageway. Perhaps that was why Groves became only slowly aware of that odd subterranean rumbling, a murmur sounding a level deeper than he had so far penetrated, a vague distant bubbling somewhere below him. He stopped and listened, then crouched down at a place where the cave wall met the floor in a cracked and pitted shelf. He put his ear there, listening, and smelled the rising dampness, like some ancient impersonal rot in the stone itself. He heard the sound of waters flowing away endlessly in the darkness far beneath him. And it was as he struggled to his feet, mentally dazed by this experience, and struggling under the weight of his heavy pack, that his light flashed on the strange cocoonlike bundles hanging down from a jutting finger of rock on the cave wall opposite.

He stood in his tracks, gasping, and noticing how the objects had been carefully strung along the cave wall. He counted them,

8

thirteen in all. He moved to get at the first one, eager to touch it, to tear it open (it looked a bit like a dark haunch of ham, he thought), then caught himself. Carefully unpacking his cameras, he photographed everything in sight. Only then did he lay hands on the first of the bundles.

It was a parcel of the softest lambskin. Inside was a single nearly blackened leg of smoked goatsmeat. Furiously, he unpacked the bundles, one by one. In each was a single leg of the goatsmeat in the same state of crumbling half-decay — in each except the last. When he unpacked the last, he was so excited it seemed his pounding heart might beat its way out through his chest. Inside the last skin was a small flat object carefully wrapped in an opaque plastic cover. The plastic, which seemed quite new, was folded in at the edges. Before he unwrapped it his trembling fingers already knew what it contained. Somehow surely but quite unaccountably, it was a book.

He turned it over, reading the title again and again, absolutely dumbfounded. Then he began to laugh. His laughter increased in volume and tumbled through the cave like a wild magnetic current. Soon it seemed that the laughter was not his but the cave's, the hidden river's, that the laughter itself had pursued him for a long time only to catch him out then and there. It went on and on. His hand shook. He dropped the book. It lay at his feet, an ordinary paperback edition of Lobsang Rampa's *The Third Eye*.

It was weeks later when Yengla brought Lord Hutton and Evans the news of the disappearance of Harry Groves. He had tracked the explorer everywhere, Yengla affirmed, into the deepest caves, and found nothing, no trace of the man, of his camp or of the two ponies that he had kept with him after Yengla's departure.

A gloom settled over the camp, and for the first time in his life the normally imperturbable Hutton began to entertain fears of ultimate failure. Everything, it seemed, was ending at last; all the possibilities imagined as part of the world they had known would have to remain unrealized.

After a few days of indecision, they agreed to continue their northwestward trek, detouring slightly where necessary to obtain some news of events in the world outside.

The day before their departure Hutton undertook a climb up the Malduk. Their camp had been made far below a labyrinth of moraine-ridges, pyramids and ice-clefts that sprang out of a great steel blue glacier on the mountain's southern flanks. Hutton climbed up toward the Kamruk glacier, which he had explored ten years before as part of a vain effort to reach the summit. On that expedition his closest friend, Ismail, a Circassian, had fallen to his death when a rope broke a few thousand feet from the very top. The body was never found.

Hutton, six feet five and proportionately muscled, a former amateur boxing champion, had studied mathematics in Berlin and had become the first experimenter to run the test devised by A.M. Turing to determine whether the then most advanced series of computers could be said to think. The tests proved inconclusive and the world ban on ultra-automation diverted work on super-intelligent machines into secret projects, the results of which were so far unknown. It occurred to Hutton, however, that the pattern of international breakdown experienced during the last several months had something predictable and almost mathematical about it. It might be that men had secretly decided, or been secretly compelled, to programme Armageddon, leaving nothing to chance or the mercies of human improvisation. It was due to his interest in the ultra-intelligent computer that Hutton had been led in pursuit of the Yeti. He had felt that if man had already proved that there was a further evolutionary stage beyond him, that of the machine, it might throw additional light on his nature if it could be proved also that there was a stage *behind* him, in the direction of the animal kingdom from which homo sapiens had partially emerged. To Hutton, the Yeti was a possible missing link in the metaphysical chain that led from unthinking matter to universal mind.

As the day passed and Hutton continued his climb, he knew that he must spend a night on the mountain, to commune with the spirits of his dead companions and to rethink some of the assumptions that had occupied him through an active and productive life. On a small outcropping of rock which fenced the glacier gorge on his right, he leveled the ground and set up his tent. Far below, the glacier tongues and lakes were already darkening, the wind stirred, and he was glad of the shelter of the few schist boulders around him as he prepared to face the oncoming night.

He had expected a picturesque sunset, but that evening it was nothing out of the ordinary. The sun sank into clouds illumined by a fiery yellow flare, which glowed for a long time after the sun had gone down, and threw all the surrounding peaks into sharp relief. Soon his tent was shrouded in darkness. For a moment the top of Malduk glittered almost as if it were an active volcano and then the light of day was swallowed up entirely.

Hutton walked out to see the full moon rise and watched it dim the stars which only moments before had glittered so fiercely. It was not so far, after all, to the boundless realms of space. The moon rose like a burnished silver shield, sailing up from the black perpendicular wall of the glacier's near defile. Everything was silent except for the occasional dull crack of a newly forming crevasse or the crash of an avalanche tumbling down suddenly from an ice-mantle higher up. It was very cold, but not punishing.

Hutton took from his pocket the book which he carried with him everywhere, a battered old copy bound in a protective jacket of *My View of the World* by the twentieth century physicist, Schrödinger. Hutton had no need to open it to the passage he wanted, for he knew it by heart. It was Schrödinger on a mountain on the Alps, confessing to himself the truth of Vedanta, that the moment was eternal, that he had always been just there and would never be anywhere else, that change was the real illusion and not permanence.

The great explorer fixed his gaze upward and outward at the moon and the silver peaks. He felt already that he was a vast distance from the earth. If he stood there long enough and patiently enough, the avalanches would thunder down toward him, but never reach him, the mountain would shift and change but stay fixed in place, the Yeti would be discovered and yet continue to be a mystery.

As the moon rose ever higher — rises ever higher — Lord Hutton is turning to point a mittened hand at the darkness. He is remembering how he once watched two Tibetan monks release the spirit of a dying man by those powerful magical exclamations that would send the immaterial soul flying into its next rebirth. Perhaps the world itself is now in need of just such a release. If he concentrates his mind and utters the magical words, standing there on that high ledge in those great spaces saturated by moonlight, perhaps he can ease the dying planet's death-agony and send everything whirling off into another dimension of space and time.

Lord Hutton raises a mittened hand at the darkness. He is trying very hard to concentrate the whole power of his mind.

HIK PHAT! he cries out, the words of the ritual exploding in his throat. *HIK! PHAT!*

Above him and around him the glacier dissolves and condenses like a sinister plasma. . . . . .

A week later Evans, quite alone, struggles on through a snowy wasteland. Every now and then he stops to fire a gun into the air, he stops to take a photograph, he stops to laugh at nothing, he stops to think.

Evans the handyman, Evans the relative of Scott's doughty companion, must remain undaunted by every circumstance. For days the skies had been full of green and gold and violet menace, the menace of unnatural beauty, and there had been no rumours because he had met no one, but rumours were now unnecessary. There was a peculiar stillness, a curious lack of vibration in the air that possibly told the story. And the strange cloud shapes of unnatural fire. And the body of a Tibetan shepherd in his tent, his features twisted hideously out of shape, as if he had looked on that unnatural fire. And the footprints everywhere, the footprints that Evans must follow higher and higher into the mountains, footprints that were neither man nor known animal, the twentieth, twenty-first, twenty-second and twenty-third attested footprints of the Yeti.

'It is curious that I am here,' Evans thought to himself, somewhere along the way. 'That I am chosen to survive to this.'

But he did survive and remembered his days in the navy, as an engineer on H.M.S. *Cobra*, sailing past the lovely harsh island of Socotra, thinking about dragon's blood trees and writing letters to his wife and four children back in Bristol. His family must be gone now, everything must be gone, but one had to do one's duty, one had to continue. It wasn't probably the fault of the machines as some people thought. It wasn't anybody's fault. It was predestined, all of this. And besides, it was never the end. There were always a few left over, to start the whole thing up again.

He chewed away on his last remaining plug of tobacco, ate a chocolate bar or two sometime later, took a swig of brandy from the hip flask. As far as he knew he was headed south toward India, over the last high peaks of the Himalayas. There was no way, of course, that he could make it, now that Hutton was gone and the porters had all deserted. But he had to go on anyway.

He came at last to a high valley in the Himalayan foothills, a broad spacious valley where the weather was milder and the snow was beginning to melt. With his food gone and his mind confused by sheer motion and by his reflections on the depressing events of the expeditions, Evans' will to live was sinking rapidly, despite the easier circumstances of travel. That night he had no strength to set up his tent. He lay down in the snow, well realizing that to fall asleep unsheltered in those temperatures would probably mean death.

The next morning he was surprised to see how much better he felt. He opened his eyes on the clear sunlit day, on a sky of blue splendour. He tried to sit up.

Then he noticed that in attempting to sit up he had somehow propelled himself up and away not only from the earth, but from his own body, which lay there inert and seemingly lifeless in the drifting, melting snow.

How curious it was to stare down at his own dead body, to see himself for the first time, when he was really no longer himself! He regarded his mortal husk with tender love and pity and wondered if he would ever again inhabit that frail carcass.

Then, slowly, like a child first learning to walk, he stepped across the snow, out and away from the scene of his own apparent death.

He moved easily across the brilliant landscape, not wanting to wander too far, wondering just what he might do next. He had heard of people who had somehow become detached from their bodies, but of course they had always managed to climb back on board, so as to tell the tale. But if he ventured back into that seeming derelict, he wondered, would this bright feeling vanish? Would he be dead and obliterated once and for all, trapped in the deep frozen hulk that such a short time before he had treasured as his dearest possession?

Since he did not know what to do he merely stayed there, keeping watch on his own body, and soon he noticed a very curious thing. Somehow time itself had shifted and became distorted, because as he waited and watched, day and night began to alternate in a strange rhythm that seemed to have nothing to do with the world as he remembered it but which responded directly to what he felt in his own mind. Before long he was making the sun and moon dance forward in crazy rhythms that were both dizzying and altogether delightful.

The next time he looked down at his own late body it had changed beyond recognition. For one thing it was much longer, at least seven or eight feet tall. Then too it had grown a thick coat of hair, a warm fur that seemed to have burst out of the crumpled and rotted clothing and which shone with vitality and health. His fingernails and toenails had become sharp curved claws on powerful extremities. His arms were longer and reached to his knees. His ears lay close to his skull, which was larger and squarer, a huge cranium covered with glossy fur.

He knew that now he could enter his body again and he did so without fear. He lay down inside himself and became one with what he had become.

When he got up, he sensed that everything had fallen back into

13

something like the rhythms he vaguely remembered. At the same time, it was very different. He stretched his arms and felt the power surge through them to the sharp curves of his magnificent claws. He could see the snow in a thousand subtle variations of line and texture. When he moved he covered the ground easily in powerful strides, and when he ran he barely touched it, bounding from place to place on an energy he drew from contact with the earth itself.

Time passed and he learned to run on the highest peaks, to cross the glaciers, to reach the caves far back in the mountains where he could exchange knowledge without words with others of his kind. Slowly, he forgot almost all of the past. He lived in the present exclusively, in the strength of his seemingly tireless pleasure.

Only once, a long time later, did he meet any creature other than his own kind, or come upon animal other than sheep or yak, wolf or antelope or bear. He was striding across a great ridge below Nanda Devi when he happened suddenly upon a medium-sized animal slipping and sliding awkwardly across the rock in tiny, timid steps. The creature, wrapped tightly in its protective garments, peered at him with a sharp and metallic gaze from behind something it wore over its face. Even in his quick sideways glance, and despite the masked face, he sensed at once its sharp curiosity, the cold hunger of its stare, the anxious struggle in that intruder between fear and awe and violence.

He bounded away gladly, leaving behind only a faint track of footprints that the wind came down and obliterated one by one.

Captain Flynn

I n an old house, part of an estate not far from the famous European town, she met Captain Flynn.

Because she had been told to, she had taken her clothes off, but her tiny bare white feet stirred up no dust, even when she moved from the polished wood floor to one or another of the thick oriental carpets that made pleasant islands between the mirrors and the shapely divan.

Standing on the central one of these carpets, and looking south, she could see through the double glass doors into the orangerie, where faint, moist blooms stretched and wavered in the spare sunlight. Turning her head to the right, she could look on the painting of the serpent and wonder at the way its arched diamond body seemed to have been nailed or rather jewelled into the paneled wall. In this same position, out of the corner of her right eye, she was aware of the mirror behind her aiming back at her some semblance of her own flesh, quite white in this aspect, twisted and poised there, as if held in readiness for something. Looking to the left, finally, she could survey the very long low soft pink sofa, a generous but palpable lotus, on which floated the still sleeping splendid naked body of her host, Captain Flynn.

If it had been up to her, probably, she would have continued staring straight ahead, for the orangerie was certainly full of pleasant shades and highlights enough for any eye, and the longer she looked the more clearly she could distinguish one beauty from another there. For example, several thickly clustering large purple climbers caused her no end of amazement, so lush they seemed, so soft hanging and yet sturdy and profuse. And also a number of cactus-like plants with sharp angular needles and little bunches of pink flowers at the tips. And the bamboo trees and the magnolia, and a specimen that must have been one of the bougainvillea, all so intriguing!

It was not only the plants, but the sculptures in the wonderful orangerie that held her attention, at least for that little while. She could make out two of the pieces quite clearly. One was the gaunt naked figure of a man, life-sized, turned upside down and apparently crucified in that position, like St. Peter. It was a bronze sculpture, quite naturalistic, but distorted and angular, held in place by crossed quartzlike pins that supported the figure while at the same time giving the effect of crucifixion. Nearby, the cactus needles shone in a nicely calculated rhythm of continuation, and the whole area around glittered in subtle finepoint.

The other sculpture was a large sphere, possibly six feet in circumference and so transparent that it brimmed with constantly shifting beams of light. Immured dead centre in this sphere was a larger-than-life reproduction of a frog, yet so lifelike it was that it might have been a mutant giant of the species, eerily staring at her.

Luckily, they had warned her not to be disturbed by any of Captain Flynn's works of art, pointing out that though he was an eccentric he must be tolerated if only because he was so definitely one of their own. Of course she had memorized the message, and was only waiting for the proper moment to deliver it. Yet to determine that moment might be a difficult problem, given that there were no orders, not even any hints on that point from the group itself, so she bided her time, aimlessly staring out at the sunshine, the greenery and the flowers. For a while she even closed her eyes and dozed a bit, only to wake feeling quite rested, quite refreshed, not least because of the elegant little breeze that seemed all by itself to have pushed the double glass doors open. She felt this breeze along the length of her body, which seemed to have fallen into place where she stood, so that she was not tired, nor had her long beautiful legs gone to sleep when she did, nor did her lovely shoulders slump unduly, given that she herself was still very far from being a statue or a sculpture and might reasonably have complained. She could even stretch her arms with impunity and fuss with strands of her dark hair, though she knew that to move her head suddenly would have been overbold.

She was not certain how she first became aware that Captain Flynn was awake. Perhaps, despite the soft rustle of the wind among the plants, she had picked up his breathing, sharpened to a new pitch as he surfaced. Perhaps, out of the corner of her left eye, she caught some slight movement, some faint stirring of that lithe and splendid black body.

However it was, she was allowed finally to turn her head, and as

16

she did so, caught her breath to see those indolent reclining almost helpless limbs (leaning back as he was almost like the black man in Homer's *Gulf Stream*, shipwrecked) tense wonderfully of a sudden and tighten with awareness, and the head — magnificent, leonine — turn just slightly to acknowledge her presence there.

Or so she thought, and remembered that the message, if it was to be given to Captain Flynn, must be given only at his command.

Then she noticed, or noticed again, for she had indeed seen it on her first surveying glance, but let it pass, that as she turned both head and body slightly Flynn-wards, the tilting gilt mirror above that lotus couch caught her, or rather just the intimate parts of her, and held them there at eye level for the man — at least from her angle.

And at this moment he stretched himself, sending shivers through and along the couch, yawned, and opened his eyes. She waited in a sudden terror of joy and suspense, but when he stirred again he turned inward and away, so that she saw at once both the back of his head and beyond that his intelligent, perfectly formed face, in the mirror, precisely *vis-à-vis* her most tender parts.

Before she could think what to do, as if to meet her secret fears and wishes together, he was leaning forward, eagerly caressing the adjacent image of her, so it seemed, though he might have been simply yawning at the wall, at the mirror. From her angle certainly his mouth and tongue and lips were fully on her, and she could not turn back for anything, could not untwist herself, out of modesty, so great was the first inflowing pleasure she felt at the sight.

After that first little shock, it never occurred to her to wonder what in fact he might be doing, or to think about what from his angle he might be feeling. It was sufficient to watch that magnificent body twisted to reach her, the lips applied to her with a determination so eager and yet fixed that it made her forget even how to move, never mind think. Indeed, for all that time she was in no danger of even attempting to speak or of trying to see the orangerie, or of demanding an explanation of anything, because her body was slowly waking up to an intensity in which she clenched to herself all her best powers of being just what she was, until the end.

She was nearly there when, with pleasure striking notes on every pulse and her thighs rubbery fine, she saw in her straight ahead fixed gaze at the wall that he moved, that he turned, that he was about to get up and possibly even come toward her! Rolling unsteadily and yet blithely as she was across a series of crests toward some unimaginable climax, she felt this as cruel indifference, even as a deliberate insult, as a terrible mockery of the complete and open intimacy she had freely given up to now, despite his failure to reassure her by even so much as a wink. He had lain there, it seemed, taking his pleasure with her in his fashion and now he was cutting out at the very moment she had dreamed of for so long, in dreams which she had refused to tell either her husband or those important persons who had sent her here, curious as they were about her inner life.

So angry was she, so crudely yanked away from a final pleasure so meaningful that she turned right around, raised both her arms and started to scream at the top of her lungs, against all the instructions they had so carefully planted in her for so many weeks before. Strangely, however, though the screams came tearing up from her chest through her throat and she could actually feel the emotion as a sudden gagging pressure that came near to choking her on the spot, no sound actually issued from her lips.

At that moment, too, Captain Flynn completed the act of getting up, and stood quivering in every muscle just in front of the pink swell of the sofa. For the first time he actually looked her directly in the face, while her glance ran angrily up and down the splendid, gleaming length of his body, slicked now with the sweat of heavy exertion. All of a sudden, it seemed, he recognized her, his eyes rolled helplessly, his body, tensed with a sullen fire of sexual arousal, dimmed and flattened before her eyes, and roaring, half in pain and half in anger, he shouted at her:

"There was no word you could have spoken. . . . . None!"

Then with a wild shamanic roll of his eyes, he whirled before she could even attempt to speak and with one strong black fist smashed the gilt mirror in pieces, falling as he did back over and across the sofa's bright pink folds, falling away into the darkness, into the unreadable dark space that suddenly loomed there.

And she, for her part, seeing him fall, and knowing indeed that there was no word she could have spoken, let herself go, collapsing even where she stood. Helpless there on the rug, she felt the strength running out of her, her rubbery thighs spread around her own dark centre that she could not even see because in falling she had turned away, not only from him, but from herself. And as she lay there, she saw the snake unpin itself from its jewelled captivity and slowly slither down the wall. She heard the wrenching away of the pins and knew that the crucified man too was waking and coming to life, and in a minute would probably enter through the double doors and find her. And then she heard the unmistakable explosion of glass that was not the door but the sphere in the orangerie. A cold, damp odor, as of the deepest earth, pervaded the room, and she heard the pleasant gigantic croaking and irregular padded leaps of the frog, which, before she could move or complain had settled its large webbed feet on her breasts, fastening itself to her with a clammy grip, while it stared down at her with its shining bulbous eyes.

It stared and stared and she could not scream but she remembered one or two of the things they said might happen to her, if she failed in her visit to Captain Flynn.

Famine

Before their fight the Craig brothers had lived together for nearly twenty years on the desolate scrub farm just beyond Hayley's pastures.

It was Garnett's farm really—he was the eldest, and after their father's death he had moved back to those rocky seventy-five acres with his new wife while Walter was still in the service. His wife was an old-fashioned woman, tall and straight and beautiful, and she hadn't minded the lack of comforts—the worn linoleum, the woodstove, the dirt and the well drying up too often, but when he began to beat her, she went sullen. How it had all happened, he could never figure out exactly, or even remember. But sometimes pictures of her came back to him and he saw her crouched in the corner of the old bedroom, her white fingers clutching tight at her shift as she wept, refusing to let him touch her. Then he had found himself striking at her, as if some anger pushing up from his belly had exploded in his clumsy hands.

After six months, her father came and took her away, warning him not to try to get her back. The old man was a tyrant, known to be quick with his shotgun, and Garnett did nothing, not even going to town any more, for fear of meeting her or her relatives. He drove ten miles out of the way to get his supplies in Crawford, and switched to the church there too, or stayed home on Sundays and read out loud the great bound Bible he had inherited from his mother, who had died in childbirth with Walter.

At last Walter came back from the war, with an idea of living on the land. There was a steel plate in the side of his head from one of the last battles with the Germans, but he had money and fair health. He had been in the hospital a long time, but they had finally passed him out, even though he complained sometimes of a rushing in his ears, like the sound of water he said, swishing endlessly in some big trough.

21

He found Garnett scraping along on a narrow margin. The tractor was old and there had been no replacement for the disc harrow that had been banged out of kilter on all those hidden stones; the tin on the barn roof was rusting badly and there were leaks everywhere rotting out the old beams. The crude pump that delivered water to the barn was barely functioning. Several fields were weeding up, and at the back corner the swamp had crept across the overgrown road, washing ancient daubs of cardboard and indestructible plastic from the farm dump across the old furrows.

Garnett had thinned down, it seemed to Walter, his face set and hollow, his glance bending away too often from the matter at hand. He said less than ever and shrugged his shoulders more, sliding through the house, murmuring to himself whenever the door slammed, or an animal stirred in the night, or the wind caught the edge of a loose board. He had been almost a young man when Walter went away; now he was gray-faced and old, with slouched shoulders and a hopeless air, except when he read the Bible: then his voice picked up, rising from his sunken chest to fill the disheveled rooms with the strange music of prophecy or poetry.

When Garnett looked at Walter, on the other hand, he saw a young man who had gone rigid in a waking sleep, from which he would sometimes burst with confident, impractical plans. Walter was possibly a little too fat; he had lost his ambition in learning something about the world. He hung back as much as he plunged forward, smiling to himself, but never talking about the past. He threw all the money he had into the farm almost as if he were in a poker game making a desperate bet on a bad hand.

Slowly, however, the house got fixed up. The weathered clapboard was covered with white siding; the old woodstove was hauled away and a furnace installed. Plywood panelling spread gradually through the rooms like a reassuring skin. They bought a new tractor, repaired the barn roofs, replaced the equipment, and bought some stock. A sit-down mower appeared, a snow-blower, new saws and other tools. A lawn was planted and cut and a plastic fountain set up there, next to the pink flamingos which they picked up on sale at the local hardware store.

For a few years they seemed to be making a little money. They bought a color television and a meat freezer, and a new monument for their mother's grave outside the village. There were no other relatives to spend money on, and neither of them ever went out. They didn't drink or smoke, but sometimes sat all night before the

22

TV, sipping coffee, dragging themselves out in the morning to do the chores after a few hours of fitful, uneasy sleep.

Their habits meshed surprisingly together. Like a cog and wheel accidentally matched, they made things go with a rough motion, not altogether snug. Every morning Garnett would make breakfast. It was always fried bacon with eggs and toast, and they ate after the first milking. Walter would come in from the barn and find the table spread, Garnett listening to the country music, slumped in the new pine rocker in a kind of daze, his lips moving slightly to the words of the songs.

They ate silently, the music rambling on. Walter was slower than Garnett and sometimes he would stop and tilt his head to one side, his mouth full of breakfast. He found the songs monotonous, having acquired different tastes in the army. Something about the songs annoyed him, but he didn't know how to say so without challenging Garnett. It was like the sameness of the breakfast, which he had complained about, only to find Garnett refusing to get up for three days, just lying there in the west bedroom, staring glumly at the yellowing flower print of the wallpaper which had not been replaced in the renovations because it had been their mother's. Finally Walter had had to apologize, though sometimes he crept downstairs early, while Garnett's snores still sounded through the hall, and stuffed himself with cheese and cereal and made tea instead of coffee, because, as he told himself, it was good to have a change.

Every morning, as soon as Walter headed back to the barn, Garnett would gather up the breakfast things and begin the washing up, setting out the scraps for the dog, which he insisted be chained up every night. He would go out the side door through the old summer kitchen which was piled with trunks, to be greeted by the eager yelps of the collie as he set down the dish. Even in winter he would stand there awhile, staring out past the corner of the barn across the fields which rolled back evenly to the line of bush that marked the government lands. Then Garnett would slowly return to the kitchen and go methodically about the washing up. He was always glad to be alone, glad to have Walter out of the house. If the heat was on, he would turn it down, and turn up the music. He liked the thick-bodied voices of the country singers, especially the sad wailing of the betrayed girls, the desperate wives. He always thought of them as real people and was shocked when Walter had once shown him an article about one of the stars in a glossy magazine. It seemed ridiculous to him that people would talk about how they were making these things up and he wanted to throw the piece away, but because of the photos of the singer's legs and bare shoulders, he found it very hard. He left the magazine in the bathroom and sometimes, as he sat there, he would guiltily turn the pages, reaching out for that shining blonde hair with his fingertips and listening for Walter's footsteps downstairs as he stroked the glossy outline of a neck or thigh.

In the barn, meanwhile, Walter would feel free for a little while. He always liked to escape from the house to the steamy darkness where the warm breath of the animals licked out at him and soothed him. The barn hadn't changed much through the years and it reminded him of his childhood when he used to hide from his aunt, who took care of them, and was always vowing she would beat some sense and discipline into them. After his father had died, his aunt had moved away and the farm went over to Garnett, who later moved back from the factory town where had had a job as a night watchman. His last time in the barn before he had gone to the army, taken by a sudden impulse, he had lain in the straw and beat about himself until the pleasure came in short, swift spurts, while the animals moaned and stamped down below him. If his aunt had ever caught him at that she would have killed him. Now he was free, of course, to do what he liked. Even so, when occasionally the need came on him, he listened anxiously for Garnett's fumbling hands on the door, and a kind of dizziness seized him, as if the waters dinning quietly in his ears would burst the sides of his head.

While the money lasted, they had built up their stock beyond what their father or grandfather had ever been able to afford. Ten or fifteen head of cattle flicked their tails between the stanchions or let themselves be eased and shouted out into the big field to graze, the dog streaking around them in full yelping voice. The pigs were penned in the barn wing, grubbing and snorting. Chickens fluttered in the ramshackle adjunct, or pecked across the yard like beaked bolsters. There were even a few sheep, though the horse had been sold to help pay for the new pickup, and the freezer was well-stocked with prime cuts of meat that had been slowly seasoned in the house shed, hung up and watched carefully against the rats.

So it worked out between them, the years ran in the grooves of familiar seasons, but as usual in the country, bad times followed soon after the good.

The government, they heard on the radio, had undercut farm prices, hurting above all the small farmer, and the brothers' money began to run short as the inevitable inflation built up against them.

Walter's monthly check could barely meet their needs, and they had to cut corners to pay off the interest on all the things they had bought on credit. On Sundays they would drive over to Crawford in the afternoon to Danny and Rae's fast food restaurant, or drop in there on the way back from church, but they seldom went to the city, forty miles away, where the prices were high and they always seemed to spend more than they intended. They had never gone out much anyway, but now it was unthinkable. It would have meant buying some new dress clothes and they were not ones to put up with the noise and foolishness of the dances for that matter. To see all those women bustling about and even drinking and smoking was a prospect that frightened them, though sometimes a terrible curiosity took hold, and they parked down the road from the huge concrete pile that was the Crawford recreation centre, watching the cars zigzag in and out of the lot and listening to the half-choked surge of the music.

Wherever they strayed, though, they would eventually circle back to the farm, turning past Hayley's brick house at the corners, watching the lighted windows disappear behind them as they rolled deeper along the dirt track that snaked in through a maze of soaring birches. Past the big swamp, with its split-boled dying trees, past the scorched outline of the burned-out Kirkwood place, they came finally back to their own land, the house and barn and outbuildings rising out of the dark like the rest of the countryside, part of their familiar knowledge.

Slowly they settled in together, turning away from the world. To Walter, the past flaked off bit by bit, leaving a few bare glimpses of his unfurnished childhood. Sometimes, in the night, Garnett would hear his brother's cries surface from a dream, and know he was back in the trenches again, feeling the fire come out of nowhere to strike him down. Garnett would insist that they watch television practically all night, anything to put off being wakened by those shouts. But Walter would hate Garnett's way of slyly eyeing the full-colour girls on the screen, refusing to turn the channels to the sports, and would storm out of the sitting room to the kitchen to make himself a sandwich and tea. Garnett could never stand him being in the kitchen, and would drag himself away from the screen and come out offering to help. But Walter would go cold, clutching the large breadknife in two hands, and slicing the meat or the cheese with a vicious downward motion, so that the table shook.

After evenings like this, the brothers would not speak for days, and one winter night, after they nearly came to blows, Walter vowed to leave. But Garnett swore he would give him not a nickel to take away, and since legally everything was his, Walter could only swallow his pride and abjectly resume his share of the never-ending routine.

Thanks to their parsimonious ways, and to the well-stocked freezer and Garnett's garden, they managed to survive the bad years without serious discomfort.

While Walter killed and cured the meat and packed the freezer with neat parcels marked with crayon, Garnett every summer planted a garden inside a well-tendered space near the barn where an old building had been torn down and the soil was rich and dark.

In the garden, surrounded by chickenwire, grew all the vegetables for their table and, in good years, a few to sell—corn and potatoes, beans and peas and asparagus, cauliflower, eggplants and onions.

Garnett watched over his garden with a tender ferocity, driving the dog and cats and chickens away, wary of the tramping cattle, spraying carefully to keep the insects off the delicate shoots. In the fall, everything that could be frozen was put away, and potatoes and other things laid down in the root cellar behind the summer kitchen.

So they survived the lean times, though they grew grayer and more silent, all the harder inside as the flesh softened around them.

Then came the terrible, final quarrel.

It was a Sunday, in the middle of July, a day that rose up out of a black furnace of night in which the moon hardened like a steel disc. Walter felt the heat more than Garnett, barely forcing down the thick and viscous coffee, labouring across to the barn and back again after chores to collapse in breathless unease at the table. He could only pick at the bacon and eggs until Garnett, in disgust, swept the food off the table.

It was time for the Bible reading, and for this they moved over to the parlour, the room set aside for their meagre formal rites, untouched since their mother's death.

The parlour smelt faintly of lavender, a big square room with purple drapes drawn, a veneered divan covered in green and purple velvet, a few large chairs, and a long doilied table on which sat stately old pieces of china and the family Bible.

Stirred by the movements of their boots, dust sieved up through every coil of the decorated floor mats, only to catch fire as the heavy curtains were drawn back and daylight poured fiercely in on them.

As usual, Garnett set the Bible on the low table in front of the divan and opened it to one of several dozen places marked by elaborate ribbons.

Walter sank down into one of the big chairs, sweat rising on his forehead. He was beginning to long for the cool woods, a bath in the pond, any escape from this heat. He resented Garnett's insistence that he take part in these readings, even when he didn't want to. He stared angrily at his brother's big boney hands turning the pages, at his thin body folded up like an insect's, at the long gray-fringed balding head that was shining with light, not sweat.

Garnett ran his thin fingers across the oversized pages and looked up with sudden sharpness at Walter, as if he could feel his resistance. Then he began to read very slowly the sonorous cadences that he knew almost by heart.

He had chosen one of his favourite passages, the story of Joseph and Potiphar's wife. In a low, creaking voice, he read the story of Joseph's temptation, how God was with him when he went to the prison, how he interpreted the dreams of the prisoners, and later the Pharaoh's dream of the gaunt cows eating the fat cows, and of the scanty ears of corn swallowing the ripe ears of corn.

He read on and on in the stifling heat of the room and pictures rose out of the familiar sentences, pictures that shaped themselves in Walter's mind despite his resistance and discomfort. They hung there a moment, bright scenes from a childhood he had somehow forgotten, then dissolved slowly like jellied candy shapes in the heat.

Still Garnett read on, but Walter closed his eyes on the light, twisting his head away from the pictures that continued to assert themselves. He thought of the mockery of such things he had known in the army, a mockery hateful to him, but telling. The soft pulse of something strange sounded in his eardrums. It was the old trouble, he thought, the rolling of waters.

"Dead Sea waters," he found himself saying aloud. And then he laughed.

Garnett's voice sharpened to a rasp, but he continued, his fingers tightening on the book.

But Walter could stand it no longer. Slowly he got up, pushing free of the heavy cushions of the chair.

Garnett stopped reading and stared up at him.

"I've had enough," Walter said, the half-stifled words spilling out as he moved for the door.

Garnett stood up too, and he started to speak.

But Walter was gone, his steps a brief thunder in the hall and kitchen.

Across the yard and straight for the barn he went, toward the cool darkness. It was time for the cows to go out to the pasture. Why should he wait in the house under the threat of his brother's anger? It was time for the cows to go out; then he could rest, and escape from the heat.

In the barn, he realized he had forgotten the dog. He would need the dog to control them. He turned back to the house.

But Garnett was there, outside, staring at him, his long figure drifting vaguely toward the pickup which sat half out of the garage-shed in the boiling sunlight.

"Goddamn it then, take the truck!" Walter called at him, and spat in the dust. The dog, hearing the rare sound of a voice raised, started to bark.

Garnett turned back, a vague blue-clad figure in a glare of sunlight, tugged at by the sharp excitement of the dog's barking.

"Goddamn it!" Walter cried out, seeing that his brother would get there first, "Take the dog, then! Read him the good book, you damned mealy-mouthed rot-preacher!"

He whirled, and headed back for the barn. By God, he would let them out anyway! He would do it without the dog.

His breath came in short gasps. The sweat ran a map of blotches over his shirt.

In the barn he plunged furiously between the stanchions, swearing again and again as he kicked at the tumbled-down bales of straw.

The cows stirred and moaned uneasily. He began to drive them one by one down the low ramp and out into the yard.

Taking fright at his speed, at his anger, at the sound of hooves crashing down on the ramp, two or three baulked, kicking and rolling in the darkness until the barn shook.

Outside, the dust plumed under the terror of the bellowing cows. The dog barked a steady staccato. Then from the bottom of a wave of darkness that seemed to take hold of him and hurl him furiously against a coil of rope, Walter heard his brother's repeated screams.

He scrambled forward toward the ramp, tripped and rolled helplessly out into the blazing sunlight, the farm jigsawed around him like a landscape of fragments.

Crawling up on his hands and knees, he saw the cows at forage in the garden, tramping and dancing and squirming between the coiled-out ruin of the fence.

His brother stood white-faced, silent now, waving his arms in a crazy semaphore of anger and despair.

Walter was some time getting the dog calmed down and working, but there was no hope at all for the garden. It had only taken them minutes to reduce it to a big, squared-off run of compost.

Garnett made no attempt to help in the roundup, but trailed back into the house, drifting past Walter, the straggling cows, and the still barking dog, without a word.

The sun fell on Walter like a pressing weight, but he laughed. He could not help it. Laughter possessed him, he shook with endless, mindless laughter as the sweat poured off him, blurring his sight and splitting his vision into a tangle of fiery threads. He rubbed at his face with gnarled, filthy hands, staring down curiously at his clothes stained with cowshit, feeling the thumps of pain from a banged-up leg. He stuck his soft belly out and laughed.

At last he dragged himself into the house, into the bright kitchen where the light seemed to sing. He moved from room to room, remembering everything, the past, all the terror, the bright pictures of the good book, even those.

He went into the shower and washed himself clean, touching himself all over, then walking naked through the house with light, dripping steps. He sang to himself, to the music inside his head, to the tides of that music.

He dried his body at last with a big towel, dressed himself in his old army uniform, which he found at the bottom of a chest in the bedroom closet, and then went down to the kitchen and ate.

He took a thick steak from the refrigerator and grilled it carefully. He pried open a sealed jug of milk and drank until it ran over the corners of his mouth. Then he sat down and ate the steak slowly, savouring every bite. The heat in the kitchen was terrible, and the sweat ran off him in a shower. He laughed.

He went back to his room and began packing. He packed neatly a suitcase full of clothes, clothes he had not worn in twenty years, none of them work-clothes, and then went down to the kitchen and jammed in all the food he could carry, bread and cheese and big slices of cooked ham.

As he was leaving the house, an old straw hat set jauntily over his face, he saw the dog and remembered something. He put down his suitcase and tramped back into the house, whistling to himself. He walked slowly from room to room, taking everything in, but with no undue haste, lingering here and there—in the parlour, in the attic, in every upstairs room, and then finally, a little while longer in the room where his brother lay, quite motionless on the narrow bed, staring up at the ceiling.

For a brief moment the brothers looked at each other. Finally, with nothing spoken, Walter turned and made his way out of the room, down the stairs and back to where he had left his suitcase. He spat as the terrified, outraged dog leapt to the full chain's length, bellowing at the dust his heels raised across the yard.

It was Hayley's boy Jack, out walking six days later, who first heard the animals howling. Something in the steady, faint desperation of the sounds disturbed him, and he mentioned it that night to his father, who shrugged it off. Those Craig brothers were weird enough, God knows, the old man said. No telling what was going on over there, probably a prayer meeting likely as anything. They listened against the wind and rushing water and picked up a strange shrill terror of sound that made them stop and look at each other with uneasy hesitation.

"I guess we'd best go down," Hayley decided, and so they went, arriving just in time to save one or two of the starving animals. Three cows came out of it all right, although the pigs had killed each other in a vain effort to find food in that dark hot barn, and the sheep had just flopped down like big bloated sacks of wool. The dog, lucky for him, had slipped his collar and was gone.

What was up in the bedroom, though was something a little stronger. The police arrived, and a doctor, shaking his head and complaining about the stench and the folly. He was a country doctor but not used to this kind of thing, much.

They never did find out what had happened—why Garnett had wanted to drag all those packages of meat up to the bedroom to thaw out and rot while the animals were raising such a howl around him. Why he had torn up the family Bible and strewn it all over the house. How he could just lie there, gnawing at those foul parcels with all that noise going on. Or what possessed Walter to take himself out to the swamp in his army suit and sit there sweating and freezing and laughing himself crazy until they finally found him and took him away, suitcase and all.

There were no answers, of course, but in those parts, for a long time, it made quite a story.

Sargon and the Fabulous Guests

The mother has forgotten her new child, who once, in a moment of blinding pain, rescued her from the terror of light and touch. That was a while ago, the birth. The forgetting happened slowly.

The hospital is the first place to mention, white and fairly clean. It was in an old section of the city, a worn brick building that they had trouble getting into, because it was 2 A.M. Even though the forms were filled out and the insurance applied, the door was locked to them — to the mother, the father, and the father's mother. When they finally got in they waited while the forms were typed. The father, slightly nervous, pointed to the floor, where a few insects scurried. His mother shook her head; it really wasn't very clean. The wife was too busy with her pain to notice.

Finally, they got to the right ward. The case room was quiet, expectancies toned to a dull somnolence by the epidurals. It was like a church at night, with lights burning, except in the waiting room, which was like a bus station. In there the smoke rolled fiercely out of the teeth of four waiting Indians, and the ashtrays, never emptied, spilled butts. It was butts the Indians talked of too, the butts, bums, bottoms of all their previous children. This one would have a bum too, but not be one, with any luck. Laughter and smoke. . .

So they left the woman there, the father and his mother, in the ward, and didn't wait, because of the Indians. It was a long lying-in, and they returned many times during the next days, until the baby was born.

The boy came quietly, in dimmed light, to the mother's eye. For a moment she saw him with clear and perfect sharpness. The doctor and the midwife congratulated her. He was taken away to be weighed and was called Richard.

31

After the great effort of the birth, the mother fell sick. It was her blood, they said, the doctor had to order transfusions. She fed the baby from her breasts. It was her first baby and she was surprised that it was so light. They put her in a room with the wife of a famous football player, and the nurses said her baby was too light. The baby of the football player's wife was heavier. Its head was covered by a mesh of tangled black thin curls. Strangely enough, it had a smaller penis than her baby did.

Richard had very strange eyes. At first they seemed blue, light blue, but when you looked more closely the left eye showed traces of mottled yellow. From certain angles, the iris seemed to glow with pink or yellow light.

After the first day the mother felt that her baby knew her, and she wondered when he would know his name. She understood very little about babies, but it pleased her to call him names from the book she had bought, from which she had already chosen his real name. Some of the names were lovely: Sargon, Moses, Karna, Paris, Cyrus. But now he had his own name, so it was no good thinking of that. It was better to look at the dozen roses her husband had sent, at the rush basket in which the fruit from his mother lay all bright and glassy, though it was real fruit.

(The football player and his wife had named their baby Jason.)

The mother's sickness kept her in the hospital for some extra days. The football player came to take his wife home, laughing and joking with the nurses. The mother was well enough to read movie magazines. She read about John Travolta, and Paul Newman, and Robert Mitchum and Franchot Tone and Mary Pickford and Rudolf Valentino. Some of them were having problems, others were dying or dead, or being remembered, or forgotten. It was all in the pictures, she really didn't have to read it. It passed the time.

Finally, she could go home. They lived in a tiny second floor apartment on the other side of the city from the hospital. It was an old house divided into many units so that the landlord could rent all the available space. Though they lived on the second floor it was dark because most of the windows faced on an alley. From her kitchen the woman could see into the living room and bedroom, though sometimes the husband would go into the bedroom and shut the door, when he was practicing. Then she could not see but she could hear the falsely struck guitar chords that would occur often as he was building up the music to a genuine tune. He had bought the guitar in the sixties when he was living in a commune but had not played it for a long time. Now he would practice again, while she preferred to watch television. It made a curious counterpoint, because she watched all the talk shows, day and night, and he would then go into the bedroom to practice. So Johnny Carson would be talking to Bo Derek, or Merv Griffin to Paul Anka, or Dick Cavett to Philip Roth, and music would begin, hesitant and frail, and in the back of her mind she would wait for the flubb which would come very soon, whether the tune was "The Times they are a'Changin" or "Buttercup Girl".

During the day, of course, it was better, because he worked in the postoffice, supervising one of the machines that sorted the mail, and he seldom got home before five-thirty, and there were no shows then.

For the baby his mother had given them a crib which they put in the living room. It was one you could plug in and it would make a gentle rocking motion, so the baby would seldom cry, even when she was slow to get up to feed him. She would sometimes get up, especially during the first weeks, and push in the wallplug that turned on both the television and the rocking mechanism of the crib and make coffee. She sat drinking coffee until she was awake, which at some point happened, and then she would take the baby and feed him. He was a very quiet baby at first, hardly looking out of his crib at all, but later he seemed to get restless.

She would be watching a rerun of the Merv Griffin show and drinking coffee in the afternoon and the baby would start to cry. So she would plug in the crib, and sit watching the stray beams of sunshine from somewhere reflected oddly on his mismatched eyes. Then he would suddenly turn his head as if something had passed by but of course there was nothing. She thought it was the change of light patterns when they switched to and from the commercials.

Naturally she was quite weak after her sickness, and sometimes she would go through the whole day and not even get dressed never mind try to go out. Occasionally, in the bathroom she would stand on the scales naked and try to see herself in the small mirror, but could only get a twisted craning version of her body, which she knew had gone badly flabby in several places. Or she would sit rubbing her folded out belly, staring at the strange lines and crinkles that might have been a map for a country that she had dreamed about but not visited.

But mostly his mother would come and would sit drinking coffee in silence, watching the talk shows on which the fabulous guests strutted out, one by one, and listening to all the interesting talk about the problems of being famous and successful. She would think how wonderful it must be to find so many words and so much humour to deal with all those problems, to be so entertaining, and not to mind moving over when the next guest appeared.

As she sat there, mostly she followed everything but sometimes, especially when her husband would be trying to play the guitar in the next room, her mind sailed off she didn't know where, and she would catch herself thinking of the hospital, or about herself as a little girl, or even about her new baby and why it was born with no hair.

One thing she thought of often was the time when she was a little girl and visited the bottling factory in her town with the fourth grade class. It was a very large milk bottling factory, the kind they had in those days, a big bruised building that sprawled around the railroad tracks, and sent up great plumes of smoke from its high brick chimney. She remembered the trucks and the big entranceway and the conveyors that wound through the building like shining silver guts. And the bottles, all clear and gleaming, that jiggled along the conveyor, in an endless row, only to come rattling out of the filler so perfectly white. It fascinated her because of how it went on, that conveyor, and because of the comical busy look of the bottles, which seemed to be circling always between full and empty, but one of them she knew would be on her doorstep in the morning, so she had some idea of the part she played in it.

But of course she almost never thought of her life in the past now. She was too busy just keeping up with all the exciting new faces of the present day; she was too busy taking care of her baby that still often cried in the night. And one day when her husband came home early he found her staring open-mouthed at all the baby's clothes which she still had to wash, and wondering what to do for their dinner. What he didn't know was that she couldn't jump up and do anything right then because she was thinking of that trip to the bottle factory which had suddenly come into her mind as soon as she pressed the button to turn off the TV, God knows why.

Her husband looked at her and said nothing. She heard him getting a beer from the fridge, and heard him go into the bedroom. He came out with his guitar, set his beer on the table, and began tuning the instrument. He didn't look at the baby of course because the baby was obviously fine.

He played a bit of "Oh Susannah", but soon struck a few really bad false notes. He put the guitar down carefully and came over to where she sat, and crouching down in front of her, his face con-

34

torted with a strange kind of elusive pain, said:

"What's your name? Please tell me your name."

She noticed that he had very deep brown eyes, like hers, and wondered about her baby's blue ones. She could not think of her name when she was asked just like that.

"I'm not sure," she said numbly.

"You know it's Merle," he said.

"Yes."

He turned away in a fit of uneasy laughter which frightened her. She got up to take care of the baby's clothes, and saw her husband disappear into the bedroom. In a little while the guitar noises came from there but she couldn't recognize any tune.

That night the baby began to cry. It wouldn't stop crying when she fed it and changed it, so she gave it some gripe water and rocked it for a while on her knee, but when she tried to put it back in the crib it started to cry again. Even the mechanical rocker didn't seem to help, and she began to worry about it.

"Richard," she asked the baby, "what's the matter with you?"

Finally, the baby went to sleep with her on the sofa. Her husband didn't wake up at all during this. Dimly, she was aware of him leaving for work in the morning. She was very tired.

Just before noon the baby began to cry again and wouldn't stop unless she held him continuously. So she called the doctor, and when she couldn't reach him, she spoke to the nurse about it.

"How old is the baby?" the nurse asked in a distant, official voice.

"Nearly four months."

"You have a colicky baby, most likely. Or else he's starting to teethe in a big way. The doctor will probably prescribe some tempra drops. He'll call you as soon as he has a free moment."

By late afternoon he had not called, but the baby stopped crying. It was another afternoon of reruns, but these she had never seen. One of the guests fascinated her so that she sank down into her chair and forgot the baby, her husband, the doctor, and even that she was watching and not overhearing a conversation.

It was a man from a child agency who was telling about the black market babies. It seemed there was a lively trade in unwanted babies, that you could get a great deal of money for a healthy white baby, because of the difficulty in the official adoption. The conversation went on and on, and she listened open-mouthed.

The phone rang shortly afterward but she paid no attention. She let it ring and ring until it stopped. Her husband came home and the television ran on. By this time they had reached Sesame Street, which she never watched.

She heard her husband storming around in the kitchen, but she said nothing at all, not even when he sank down on the sofa and drank off three beers with a quick, furtive motion. A little later he went out, slamming the door.

It was very late and she was all but asleep when he came back that night, clumsy and crashing, past the sofa and into the bedroom. In the morning he left early.

After he had gone she got up very quietly to get her coffee, but as she moved across the room, watching the baby all the while, she stepped against an object that made her stop short and almost lose her balance. He had set the guitar against the coffee table and she hadn't even noticed. Slowly it sank to the floor, looking like a funny shrunken coat rack, making a hollow kind of plunk as it settled. She stepped around it gingerly to pick it up, and the baby began to cry, softly at first, as it if were crying inward into some dream, then louder as she stood there wringing her hands in helpless frustration.

Now she had no medicine for the baby, because the doctor hadn't called, or she hadn't answered, her husband was angry because she couldn't always remember her name, and her mother-in-law had gone to Florida. She hushed the baby as best she could, drinking cup after cup of coffee, not even turning on the morning shows until she had made up her mind about it and actually begun to dress him, and herself, to meet the cold morning air.

Outside, the streets were almost empty. A few cars stirred and coughed into motion, sliding out from hidden driveways. She walked up to where the bus stop was, opposite the neighborhood grocery, happy about the nice fresh pink that was creeping into her baby's cheeks, thinking how sly he looked with that strong searching glance buried deep in those strange blue eyes. Then the bus came, roaring and groaning around the corner, desolate with all its lights set against the flat gray gloom of the morning.

It was the first time she had taken her baby on a bus, and he seemed to like the motion, because he smiled up at her suddenly, almost his first real smile, and an old woman sitting opposite leaned over and began to fuss over him, asking how old he was, if he was boy, what his name was, and so on interminably until they were almost downtown and the bus began to fill up and she had to stop.

Well, it was too bad if he had decided now that he was going to be good, the mother thought. It would all end the minute they got home. He would start to cry and nobody would ever sleep and her

36

husband would blame her and nothing would ever be right. She looked down at her little boy, who had dozed off, and felt a very soft slow moving pressure as of a very gentle warm fingertip run down her right cheek, but it was only a tear.

She got out where she thought would be best, near the market, and hurried between the shabby faceless buildings, in which some old and forgotten machinery seemed to be running on to such purposes as she could hardly imagine. The market square itself she barely recognized, though she had been there many times before. Trucks and vans everywhere in motion, piled-up boxes concealing the glassy storefronts, little swirls of furious activity, and shouts in many strange languages reverberating under the dim arcade.

This was the place, she thought — where else? — but at first she didn't really know what to do next, so she wandered among the stalls that were being set up and watched the produce being unboxed — a spilling out of eggs and oranges, cauliflower, carrots, apples and bananas, making little inert splashes of color on the tables at which there were still very few buyers. Finally, she got up courage to ask one red-faced man in overalls about what she had come for, but he turned on her with a huge shrug and babbled something in a foreign language, his hands and jaws working in furious rhythms that she couldn't read. Another man came over, and she tried to make him understand, but he stood there, motionless and blank, as if he regretted a little the secret joke that was lost between them. She started then to move away, feeling altogether heavy and helpless, when a third man appeared, who seemed to have overheard, and who understood. He began to say something, sputtering and angry, then changed his mind and pointed sharply behind her, as if he were ordering her to clear out altogether.

Turning, though, she saw a narrow alley leading into the main market building, to which he might have been directing her, and she gladly went where he seemed to be pointing, afraid of making a scene over the whole business.

Inside, she walked in a glare of light between rows of shut-up boutiques, the windows reflecting in duplicate soaring ghosts that brushed across brilliant displays. All at once she was beginning to feel a kind of despair, seeing her child stir under her chin — yawning with closed eyes, snug in its carrying straps — but she kept on walking and came finally to a place where the corridor joined up with a larger inside mall. Here, in front of a shuttered store-front sat an old woman, bent over a table on which were placed dozens of antique glass bottles of various sizes.

Hesitating, she looked first at the woman, who was wrapped in a shawl, and might have been asleep, and then up and down the length of the corridor. It was cavernous and almost empty, though at one end an old man was vigorously sweeping, and at the other, someone she couldn't see seemed to be hammering on a kind of metal.

Suddenly, she realized that the woman's head had moved and that she was looking up at her with very dark, greedy, anxious eyes.

"So you've come to sell your baby?" the woman said in a flat indifferent voice, her gums rolling pink as she spoke, her shawl drawn tighter around her by a pair of scrawny, eager arms.

She did not know what to answer, but nodded helplessly, staring down at the rows of dusty bottles, feeling the woman's gaze cut through her, afraid of what she would ask next.

The old woman said nothing more, however, but with a long-drawn out groan of resignation, dragged herself to her feet, steadied her bent body for a moment against the table, and then tottered away with slow staggering steps in the direction of the man who was sweeping.

It seemed to take a long time for her to reach him, and he made no effort at all to advance to meet her, though he looked up a few times as she came closer, then finally stopped sweeping altogether when she was no more than a few steps away.

There followed a long muttered exchange between them as the mother watched from a distance, clutching her baby, which moved restlessly in her arms now, perhaps because it was listening to the wild furtive beating of her heart.

After a while the old woman turned and began the slow painful walk back. Under her arm she carried what looked like a small white plastic bag. Down the length of the corridor, the man was sweeping again, paying no attention. The distant metallic hammering continued.

She took the bag from the old woman, and opened it, feeling very nervous under the scrutiny of those black beady eyes. Inside was a frayed, worn-looking roll of bills, held together by a rubber band. Idly, almost dreamily, the mother fingered the bills. She was aware of the old woman's eager eyes on her. The bills numbered twenty, in the single denomination of a thousand dollars.

She started to say something, then changed her mind. She shoved the packet of bills into her coat pocket. The bag fluttered down to the polished floor.

Fumbling a little with the straps, she finally untangled her baby.

Richard looked up at her with a calm uninquisitive gaze. She passed him over to the old woman, turned, and ran in sheer terror back down the corridor from which she had come.

Outside, the market square seemed suddenly crowded, as if she had been away for a long time. She thought she saw the three men she had asked for directions standing over a huge barrow of apples, pointing at her and whispering together.

She kept on running for nearly the length of the block, then slowed down, out of breath, and hastily shoved the empty carrying straps inside her coat. Someone might think, if they saw those straps that she had somehow carelessly lost her baby.

But of course she had not lost it but sold it, because it was necessary to bring peace, and to make her husband happy. All the way home on the bus, she hummed a little song to herself. She felt so much lighter and happier.

When she finally shut the door behind her, the apartment seemed very dark and small. She put the coffee on right away, and just managed to catch the final segment of the afternoon Merv Griffin show. While she was watching she folded up the baby's crib and managed to get it tucked away under the bed. She threw all the baby's toys and clothes there also.

She took time making dinner, grilling a steak from the freezer, cutting up the green beans, making a soup and boiling the potatoes. As she worked, Sesame Street and the news flashed by. Her husband was very late. Perhaps he would come just before bedtime and would miss dinner. This thought made her rather sad.

It grew late and the meal, done at last, had to be held. Soon she found herself very hungry, wondering where he might be, and she began to nibble a little at the food. She ate more and more, and soon she had finished nearly everything. Still, there was no sign of him. She took out one of his bottles of beer from the fridge and drank it slowly, and still there was no sign of him. She made coffee and flipped the television around to the print-out news channel. She watched the news reel itself out, item by item, world news, local news, sports, then finally the weather. He did not come. She picked up his guitar and strummed it idly, discordantly. Finally, she opened another beer, and swallowed it quickly, together with a handful of pills.

She woke up feeling very ill. There was no sign of him. The television continued to unfold the printed news in sharp white letters against a bright red background. It went on and on, the same stories returning, sometimes a little changed. The shifts were imperceptible. She understood nothing of it. She tried to sleep.

He did not come back that day or the next. She lay on the sofa, thinking of nothing, sometimes changing the stations. She watched even the fabulous guests from a great distance of hunger and pain. All their talk, all their wonderful sentences, rolled on her eardrums, like strange voices she had heard as a child on the edge of sleep, almost soothing. Their smiles touched her brow like feathers. She got up and stood in the kitchen, chewing on a few stale slices of bread, then lay on the sofa for a long time staring at the ceiling.

On the third day, when a vision of her child crept slowly back into her mind, and she thought that she might just get up and make sure of the money, her husband returned.

He arrived before dinner time, and edging into the room with a nervous smile, he pulled the door closed without turning, his hands behind him on the doorknob, hidden. She lay there staring at him, unable to say anything. Slowly, he surveyed the room, the disorder, the blaring TV, her listless form on the sofa. Then, without a word, he went into the kitchen and she heard him open and then slam the fridge door. She heard the pop of the beercap, and he appeared again, a beer bottle in his right fist.

"I was on a trip," he said.

"I sold the baby," she said.

The beer bottle seemed to fall slowly, so slowly she could almost read the label. It bounced on the rug and the beer gurgled out in a thin plume of froth.

He saw at once that she was telling the truth; he had missed something in the room and now he knew what it was.

He opened his mouth, a loud howl seemed to tear him apart, yet to remain outside him, as if it had found him standing there by chance.

Then he could not stay still. Up and down he went, pacing the length of the small apartment. He disappeared into the bedroom, immediately reappeared, and walked the length of the place to the kitchen. He repeated this pattern in ever quicker motions until he was almost running.

At one point he stopped and picked up his guitar. He stood there, his hands striking wildly at the strings, but it made no sense.

Later, she brought him some of the pills. He took a handful and lay on the sofa groaning.

The next morning he would still not get up, but took more of the pills, washing them down with several bottles of beer. She decided she would have to try to find the child and drank cup after cup of coffee until she felt well enough to go out. She had slept on the floor by the foot of the sofa because she did not like to be in the bedroom alone. She explained to him what she intended to do.

Soon after she slipped out of the apartment, the money stuffed into her coat pocket. She left the television on to cheer him up.

She took a taxi straight to the market. The driver tried to make conversation but she had nothing to say and he soon ignored her. But he did say it was foolish to rest her head against the window, and then drove on with a kind of vicious recklessness. She paid no attention.

The market was already crowded. She had arrived rather late. When she got to the inner arcade, the old woman was nowhere to be seen. She ran up and down in a panic, staring into each shop in turn. Many were still shut up tight, but in others salespeople behind locked doors prepared for the coming day, flitting about between the counters like animated mannikins. After a while she was exhausted and collapsed onto a bench among some stringy half-withered plants. In despair she leaned back, shutting her eyes.

When she opened them, she saw, through an angle of yellow leaves, the old man sweeping. She recognized him at once and ran to him. Her words poured out, a little too loudly, across the arcade. A few people turned to stare and smile. The old man listened impassively, resting on his broom, staring at her intently with his sharp little eyes.

He said at last that there might be something that could be done about it. She should make up her mind though, he said. He could promise nothing at all, but she should come back tomorrow, much earlier. He would see what he could do.

She went home wearily, with slow heavy steps. She could not bear to take the bus, to be shut up in a taxi. She moved at last with a growing fury through the alien streets.

When she got home, her husband was better, sitting up on the couch, drinking coffee. He listened to her in silence, his eyes shining with a brilliant blankness. He said they could not call the police, for fear of trouble. He himself would go in the morning. He would do what he could, he said in a sinking voice.

They sat up all night, drinking coffee. From time to time, he strummed his guitar, fitting new music to some words which she did not understand, making many mistakes but going always further until the song was finished.

At the first sign of daybreak he left without a word.

She waited all day in a frenzy of nervous terror. She wanted to set up the crib but could not bear to touch it, or the toys, or any of the baby's clothes.

All day she listened for his steps on the stairs, moving back and forth between the door and the window, only sometimes stopping to let the images from the television take hold of her. She wanted those colours to wash over her, to dissolve her into themselves, all those reds and yellows and blues flickering there as she fixed on them with an ever tighter ever more vicious embrace.

Later, she knelt in the bathroom, her head bent under the taps so that the stream of water struck her on the back of the neck. This was how he found her when he came in, carrying their baby.

She took the baby in her arms and held it. Water ran over the faces of mother and child.

Later, they sat before the television with the baby. The crib had been set up nearby. It rocked gently to and fro. The baby stared out at the mother and the mother stared greedily into the baby's eyes, while the man played music for the words which neither of them could really understand.

> The little boy lost in the lonely fen,
> Led by the wandering light,
> Began to cry; but God, ever nigh,
> Appeared like his father in white.
>
> He kissed the child & by the hand led
> And to his mother brought,
> Who in sorrow pale, thro' the lonely dale,
> Her little boy weeping sought.

The father played this with many mistakes, and when he was finished, she told him.

"This isn't our child," she said, in a slow deliberate voice. "His eyes aren't the same; see, they're straight blue. Those aren't Richard's eyes."

The man groaned and put his face in his hands. "It can't be," he said, shaking his head slowly. "It can't be."

"I'm going to call him Sargon," she said. "That name is in the book too. If we're to have a new child, he must have a new name."

The man closed his eyes. He couldn't think of such things anymore; he had been through too much. After a while, however, he seemed to recover a little, and they all watched television together, waiting for the fabulous guests.

At Approximately Three P.M.

The man is making peanut butter cookies. His wife comes into the kitchen. She's been reading Virginia Woolf and typing up her dreams. She stands there, on the other side of the round oak table and begins to speak. He's aware of how beautiful the day is, winter sunlight flaring up suddenly through the pines, striking the snow to countless fine-points of crystal. Through the newly installed sunroom doors he can see everything, it's all just as they planned, and already a lot brighter in the old stone house.

The woman begins to speak in a crumpled voice. Their child comes into the room with some blocks. He asks in his two-year-old way for his TV programs but it's far too early, only three o'clock. He drops the blocks and says something incomprehensible about the carpenter who's been working on the bathroom panelling but has just now gone off for material. The sunlight continues to pour itself out.

The woman is explaining to the man that she is nearly at the breaking point. They've lived together eleven years and she's always been miserable, she tells him. Her face is tight, and her voice faint and edgy. She'll have to go away, she explains, to take some kind of rest cure, she is so unhappy. The man puts the final touch, the vanilla, into the cookie dough and begins to knead it and roll it out. He rolls the dough into small dollops and presses them out with a fork. She must do whatever she thinks right, he tells her in a mechanical voice. The oven has been pre-heated to 375 degrees fahrenheit. The child drops his blocks and asks for his dinosaur book. It's as if the pines are on fire now, the sunlight angling up from some deep place in the fields beyond, almost blinding.

The man begins to put the cookies into the oven, shoving the trays in together and checking the temperature. The child ransacks his low kitchen bookshelf and pulls out his book about trucks.

Turning the pages, he calls out the name of each kind of truck, skipping the ones the can't remember. He pays no attention to his parents. The woman comes around the table and stands in the sunlight. She's wearing a navy blue sweater and jeans and her hands move nervously in the sunlight.

The woman explains that she may be going to have a breakdown. She has no freedom and no life with him, it is hopeless. She feels flayed every day they are together. The child looks up at his parents and comes across the room and around the table. He sits on one of the table's lionpaw legs and begins to chatter away nonsensically.

The man tells the woman that she should discuss this with her analyst. He says she's probably just drinking too much coffee. Then he turns to check the first batch of cookies, noticing sunlit crumbs on the bare hardwood floor.

The woman loses control and begins to scream. The man is alarmed and tries to brush past her. She swings out at him with a closed fist and deals him a sharp blow on the back of the neck. The child grabs hold of his mother, whimpering loudly.

The man feels the pain ringing out in his shoulders and neck. It's a clear signal, and makes him aware of himself. He's very nervous and cannot stop laughing. He thinks he may have been laughing before, when he mentioned the analyst and the coffee. He points frantically to the child and asks her please to control herself.

The woman controls herself with an effort. Every expression squashed now from her face, she picks up the child and sits him up on the table. The sunlight makes a gold-haloed fringe around his fairy-tale locks.

The man realizes the cookies are burning. It seems he has only just put them in the oven, even so, they are burning. He opens the door quickly, with the frayed old oven mitts, and pulls the smoking trays out. The cookies are burnt black and at the same time soft. He touches one and it makes a brown smear on the mitt.

The woman puts her son down and collapses into a chair. She sits staring straight ahead into the sunlight. The man carries the cookie trays to the sunroom door and slides it open. A chill breath touches him. He throws the cookies away into the snow. A black cat runs out from under the porch and begins to paw at the cookies. The man closes the door and turns to the woman, not touching her. The child runs to the glass panel to look at the cat. The cat begins to eat the cookies.

The man sees the carpenter's truck returning. It stops in the driveway and the carpenter gets out. His breath is steamy in the air.

44

He picks up his toolbox and some wood from the truck and comes to the door. The child turns away from the cat and runs to the door to greet the carpenter. The man opens the door.

The woman's head sinks slowly down on the table, as if she might be falling asleep. Her breathing is regular, solemn. The carpenter starts carrying his wood into the kitchen. The child plays with the wood.

The man sees that their Husky has come to chase away the cat and to eat what's left of the cookies., The dog rubs its silver-gray fur on the darkening snow.The man thinks of putting on a record to cheer things up, because he knows it will get dark very quickly now. Instead, he pours himself a small glass of brandy and goes into the other room to sit down before the fire. After a while the child comes to join him. It's time now for the child's programs and the man turns on the television.

The woman lies motionless, sprawling across the table. The carpenter does not go upstairs to finish the bathroom. He begins to work right there in the kitchen, sawing and banging and drilling as the sun sinks lower and lower and finally disappears. The man comes into the kitchen and turns on the lights. He sees his own reflection in the sunroom windows. When the carpenter finishes his task the man helps him lift up the woman. They lay her gently down inside the coffin. Her eyes are closed now and her breathing has stopped altogether. They stand there for a moment looking at her. The man is trying to remember whom to call. In the other room, the child begins to laugh and sing.

The Medium

Inside the cabin, lulled by the pleasant piped-in music, Dr. S., the well-known television scientist, dozes and waits for the miracle of flight. He is thinking, perhaps for no reason at all, of a fox he once saw on the farm of a friend at dusk. The fox, sharp red against the spring green foliage, turned for an instant to look at him just before it vanished into the gathering shadows. That look, he knew, was the inside-out of nature, and he couldn't read it. He had forgotten such looks in taking stock of the glances, rubbery or brittle, directed at him daily by his fellow humans. They recognized him, of course, but couldn't always remember from where. And soon he waited for and was amused by that recognition, partial or otherwise. He even missed it when it was lacking for more than a few hours, though it seldom was, because he spent most of his time these days (and nights) in airplanes, between engagements, most of his life in the functional plush of cabins exactly like this, or in the functional clutter of studios. (From there you looked at nature outside-in, hoping to catch the gleam in the eye of the fox).

Now the engines of the plane roar well and truly; there is a slight shiver, and, barely perceptible, the hoarse mechanical whisper of hidden parts. The attendants have been busy, assisting a spastic, handing out newspapers and candy, unpacking food and drink. They have noticed their notable passenger obliquely, if at all. Eyeing his briefcase, Dr. S. sighs and prepares to take aim at his scripts.

Concentration, however, does not come. The plush cabin soothes, without releasing, the stranded senses. A moment's self-reflection, with ominous logic, beams up Narcissus. Dr. S. retraces his steps through the waiting room, past the boarding desk, and into his seat, re-arranging the fleeting faces to restore a pattern from which he can mentally check out all the various reactions to his own presence. At the same time, he is struggling with one part of his mind to remember how Bohm's use of the hologram illustrates the notion of implicate order, that order out of which everything that is emerges. Dr. S. reaches for his briefcase. SCIENCE EXPLAINS. (Why hadn't he followed that fox into the woods, he wondered? Perhaps the sharp glance was a warning. But of what? His own dog, Quantum, was incapable of such a glance. In the strictest sense, Quantum was hardly "natural" at all).

The plane sits poised in its loop of space-time, shuddering, then at the peak of its shudder, rolls forward. A sudden thrust, a steepening angle of climb. They are strung now on a line of invisible points and headed west for the city of the angels. Why is it, Dr. S. asks himself, that I always think of death at these moments of absolutely routine miracle? He swallows very hard, his body tense and straining upward as if to fly out of the coffin that the plane might become. As usual he recognizes the ironies of all deaths accompanied by bad food, second-rate movies and superficial conversation. But the roar reassures, the angle of climb becomes normal. A few moments more and there is a general release of tension, a general rush to fall into the lazy banalities of travel.

Up the wide aisle, suddenly, myopically, trots none other than Harmon Yablonski, the famous neurological specialist from McGill. The famous neurological specimen, thinks Dr. S., watching the nervous flutter of hands, the jerk of the shoulders. Yet he responds amiably, automatically to the curt nod, with a benevolent, bare-toothed smile.

Suddenly, the aisle is crowded, as the captain's blurred voice dispenses from above a few facts about the weather and altitude. Orange-red sunlight enters a tangle of bodies edging gently tailwards, giving their movement an air of intention, as if they were dancing (And this environment, our world, when you think of it, thought Dr. S., is one that tries to simulate order, if only to pretend to banish all chance. It is precisely the opposite of the forest path, where the fox may suddenly turn and look at you, for no reason you could easily fathom. And even if some crazy hijacker sits in the third seat forward with bombs strapped to his belly, the machinery that works against him will be relentless, and quite predictable. Which is the beauty of human technology, and its terror).

Dr. S. has scribbled some of this in his notebook. The innocuous-looking lady in the green blouse who sits opposite leans over.

"Haven't I seen you on the Merv Griffin show?" she asks.

48

Her confusion of him with George Hamilton or Chevy Chase or Carl Sagan settled, she turns the talk to the most recent issue of *Astrology Today*, which she carries in a very large string bag, with some oranges and her knitting. Her interest in quarks and quasars is certainly limited, but she is anxious to talk about the stars. She tells him she is Mrs. Fox from Cinncinnati.

Dr. S. order another drink and turns to his neighbour on the left. This turns out to be merely a Mr. Neumann from Des Moines, solid and red-faced, brusquely shifting pages of the *Wall Street Journal*. He soon confides that the gold shares he bought last year now seem to be much more of a liability than an asset; he is waiting for some world crisis so that he can sell the damned things off at only a small loss, he confesses — but not too big a crisis.

Now drinks are being served right and left, ensuring the friendly glitter of ice aloft, the warming conversations. The plane climbs safely, boldly up through a plateau of clouds. From a cosmic perspective of course it has barely unsnuggled from earth. A few children gasp, and then whine as the unimaginable boredom of the experience takes hold; everyone else sinks down routinely into business or pleasure. Dr. S. finally turns his attention to one of his scripts.

2.

Through the very same sky that the plane sweeps, through the crowded indiscrimate atmosphere, shoot images from all directions, including several rebroadcasts of Dr. S. explaining science to everyone who cares to listen and watch. Through various regions, encabled or afloat, the discussions continue, as station after station goads the public into awareness of the latest discovery, the neatest invention.

Out of Nashville, Dr. S. is explaining the heart's magnetism, the powerful field around that organ, complete with diagrams, animations, colour simulations, and remarkable photography of someone's actual pumped-out life's blood. From time to time S. intervenes, or his voice-over highlights the slow-motion, running breathing segments of people, their energies monitored, charted and measured. (In the control room technicians are watching the tape and sipping coffee).

Out of Chicago, Dr. S. is explaining how animals may predict earthquakes. Here are close-up photographs of the sensors of hammerhead sharks. A flock of pigeons rising then suddenly crashing down on a barn. A special graph comparing the auditory range of man with that of mice and bats. Spectacular footage of Mt. St. Helen's. As always, the faces of eager and serious scientists.

Out of Toronto, Dr. S. is talking about butterflies. Pictures abound. Numbers and commas, exclamations and question marks materialize on the shimmering wings of the insects. Bright colours concealing poison discourage some predators, the same jeweled brilliance in certain habitats dazzles, conceals. Dr. S. and his cameras document patterns, pinpointing signs without codes.

The plane drones into darkness, crossing weather systems, seismic zones and the continent's wild geography. Mrs. Fox, discovering he is a Pisces, lets S. down easily. It's really a terrible year for that sign, as she knows, but she doesn't say so. She covers up the news with encouraging hints about personal challenges, only confirming by her vagueness the distrust S. feels toward her pseudoscience. Yet since he's had more than one drink by now he accepts her rambling reports with some tolerance. The businessman, an Aries, is drawn in. She tells him to sell off his gold without fail. Well-dressed, smoothly polished, with a touch of paunch, the man reminds S. of a cabinet minister he once interviewed.

As the relevant stewardess, a born-again Christian, and strangely enough, a Gemini, delivers his dinner of roast beef and lukewarm potatoes, red wine and peach compote, she too is tempted to start up a conversation with the famous scientist. For years she has faithfully watched S. unfolding miracle after miracle, taking note with him of the promise of this new discovery or that, while sadly suspecting that he may have forgotten God. She is very anxious indeed to ask him about this possibility, but restrains herself, not being sure that her airline training program would encourage it.

S. watches her skillfully remove the remains of his half-eaten inedible compote. He has been trying without success to get his tape recorder working, and after the coffee and brandy, as his neighbours begin to sink down into leaden half-consciousness, he finally asks her about the problem.

"It's important that I listen to these recordings and interviews before we get to L.A.," he tells her, though of course it isn't.

Down its whole length the cabin has sunk into darkness, a few of the reading lights private as candles, unwinking. The stewardess takes the faulty recorder and tries it again and again, but apart from the hiss of the reel there is nothing to be heard. Finally, however, she locates what sounds like something, a few wild whines and growls, and hands the recorder back with a smile that tells her famous passenger she is glad to have been of service.

50

As she moves quickly off, Dr. S. listens in perplexity to what ought to be his half-hour interview with a Florida scientist, the latest to become well-known for his studies of dolphin behaviour. The interview has been processed in the Florida studio as a check on the video portion. All that comes over now though is a wild flurry of whistles and screeches, punctuated by a hissing silence.

"God, I hope the video didn't screw up too," he murmurs out loud, turning for sympathy to Mrs. Fox across the aisle.

She, however, like Mr. Neumann at his left elbow, has fallen fast asleep.

3.

The plane wings on through the night. All around it, from the darkened countryside, a network of dreams. In the cabin a few filaments gather, then dissipate quickly. The patterns remain unsuspected, dreams interlocking in vast networks, of which only a few signals flicker briefly in the single mind.

Dr. S. dozes, then nods off to sleep. He dreams of a fox which turns to stone as he looks. As he reaches down to examine it a voice cries out, warning him that it may be rabid. Someone tells him then that he is on the air. He cannot speak but pitches backward through a cloud. He falls, seemingly hundreds of feet. As he is about to smash into the ground, he wakes up, feeling very cramped in the legs and more tired than before.

The sun drills up from the eastern sky, the cabin is astir. Coffee is served. Mrs. Fox from Cinncinnati chooses tea and after a little while seems to be reading the leaves. Mr. Neumann from Des Moines goes off for a walk and a cigarette. S., on his way to the toilet, runs into Yablonski, who nods and mumbles something incomprehensible. Breakfast is served and the general chatter swells. S. has another try at his tapes; he is getting advice from right and left now but nothing works. The stewardess is even more sympathetic, but this time the tape seems quite blank; there is nothing at all to be heard. S. meanwhile is finding the stewardess rather attractive, and is determined to keep in humour despite this little technical failure. He asks her to dinner at Garibaldi's, his favourite Los Angeles restaurant. She is overjoyed, realizing that she may be able to talk to him about some of the Big Questions after all.

The plane descends to the runway, perfection. Everyone is tired but happy to be delivered safely. Passengers disperse in all directions, relieved to be released from the forced intimacies of the trip. S. makes his way to his hotel, where he showers and falls asleep, leaving word he is to be awakened at lunchtime. In the early afternoon, well-fed and rested, he takes a taxi to the studio.

The studio occupies part of a brightly ornate building left over from the Hollywood of the thirties. On its facade, an overblown gang of satyrs chase a few frowzy nymphs. Inside, the recessed lighting glitters on polished brass fixtures. S. finds his way down a marbled corridor, turns into a large suite of offices and approaches the familiar receptionist. She tells him that Mr. Allen is waiting in the projection room for him.

Allen, a short, bald man with a thick mustache, greets him warmly. Three shirtsleeved technicians are fussing over a large bank of machinery. Canisters and rolls of tape are scattered on the tables in front of them. Two projectors point in businesslike fashion at screens. S. swings his own heavy cases up on one crowded table. He flops in a chair. Allen hands him a cup of coffee and asks about the trip.

"Good," S. tells him succinctly, and then explains about the tapes.

"I can't understand that," Allen shakes his head. "There's never been any trouble with the processing from down there. Let's take a look at the video."

He signals to one of the technicians. The man fetches the tape indicated by Dr. S. The other technicians slip away as the monitor playback begins.

Everything seems to be functioning nicely. S., dressed in a sports shirt and white trousers, is standing in a bright tropical setting. Shots of dolphins are intercut with his stroll down a long beach. He continues his explanation, moving out on a finger of rock where the sea lashes wildly. The colour is perfect, the editing smooth and professional. The explanation ends with a dissolve to a medium shot of the scientist he has already introduced. The camera pulls back, revealing a very large tank. More closeups of dolphins in action. The two scientists trade comments, voice over.

"Looks good to me," Allen is saying.

Action sequence of dolphins. The voices fade out, the music comes up strong — part of *La Mer*, as suggested by S.

S. starts to turn to Allen to ask him whether the choice is too obvious. The dolphins come leaping, as if at the camera. S. stops in his seat. The dolphins leap out of the monitor, they cascade in the air, as S. jumps away.

Dolphins spill through the air. They fall, sleek bodies flopping, across the floor of the studio.

S. staggers up out of his chair. Allen does not move, but looks up at him inquiringly, a slow sideways glance.

The dolphins continue to pour out of the monitor. They cover the floor of the studio, writhing and twisting in pain. It seems they are in pain, they are beaching themselves, they are dying. It seems they can no longer breathe.

S. can no longer breathe. A choking fit seizes him, he falls to the floor, flopping and twisting in pain.

Allen jumps out of his seat and reaches down wildly for S. "What's the matter, for God's sake? Are you O.K.?"

S. rolls and writhes, helplessly scratching at sand. The sea is far away.

The technician steps forward and kills the playback. Allen is helping S. to a chair.

"Should we get a doctor?" he asks. "What the hell happened to you? Are you having a heart attack?"

S. feels himself pushed down into a chair. He stares around for a moment, blind.

"What the hell happened to you?" Allen asks again.

S. comes back to the room. He opens his eyes in surprise, and for once he is speechless. Finally, he murmurs something about jetlag, determined to get away as quickly as he can. He can see that Allen is not reassured but there is nothing he can do. For a few minutes he just sits there, breathing heavily. As he painfully gathers his notebooks and struggles out of the studio, he can see the technicians looking at him. Something sharp and blank in their gaze makes him think of the fox.

He taxis back to the hotel and goes straight to his room, where he lies down on the bed without undressing. He stares at the ceiling for a while, then he closes his eyes. He does not sleep but a little later feels the need to talk to a colleague. Bronowski is dead, so he tries to reach Carl Sagan, but he is told Sagan is busy doing a talk show. He tries to reach David Suzuki, who is even then being interviewed by *People Magazine*. He calls Allen and tells him he plans to take a few days' rest. He calls the stewardess and tells her he cannot meet her for dinner. He hangs up the phone knowing full well he will stay in the room for some time. He lies down on the bed. It grows darker as he lies there. He does not turn on the television.

Massenet and the
Disappearing Sopranos

Whose life is ever complete? Events make distant echoes and the past is continuously replayed, even for the dead. The composer we know as Jules Massenet, famous for his sentimentally appealing operas, and his fondness for beautiful sopranos, died in 1912. What follows takes place partially in the past, and partially in a future which meets that past only as fiction, here in the form of this story.

Massenet, once again exactly forty-one years old, has just written *Manon*, that opera of male passion and self-deceit and innocent female opportunism, and as usual is awaiting at a distance the verdict of the audience of the Opéra Comique. Although he has often gone to the rehearsals of his operas, making sure that this or that detail is quite correct, and sometimes changing the score on the spot to accommodate necessity, he makes it a point out of superstition never to attend the actual premières of his own works.

Sitting comfortably at home in the village of Avon before a specially built screen, preparing to watch his new opera on the private viewing system, which gives him a perfect angle of vision on the Opéra stage, Massenet is nonetheless very nervous. The busy, quite plain maid has come and gone, leaving behind half a decanter full of a pleasant Beaujolais. Ninon, his wife, has carried her knitting away to her own room, and will no doubt make an appearance, for politeness' sake, at the perfect moment, when she is sure all is going well. Massenet decides to turn off the sound on the pre-performance chatter that will rehearse his career, his accomplishments, his failures and trials, almost as if he were a dead man. He is thinking, with some passion, of a peculiarly touching moment during those first days at Vevey, of Sybil standing against the large

55

double doors of the hotel suite, the gold, orange and pink light of a spectacular sunset pulsating around her and making her look like a flower in the centre of a cyclorama.

Sybil Sanderson he had met one evening just as he was slipping away resignedly from a boring dinner, which he had only decided to attend at the last minute.

A handsome older woman approaches and introduces herself. She is from Sacramento, California, resident in Paris; her husband, who has recently died, was a justice of the American Supreme Court. Would Massenet listen to her daughter, who is studying with Marchesi, and who, claims her mother, is amazingly talented?

Massenet is inclined to give in, noting how well-preserved is this older woman, in her deep midnight gown of gathered tulle—a shapely stately woman, who speaks French with only a slight and charming accent. But when he sees the daughter, the composer melts: she is very young, and extraordinarily beautiful, with such lovely skin and such dark-flowing, gold-toned hair, gestures that strike deep and transfixing eyes. (It is nothing that now and forever, thumbing through the many biographies written after his death, the composer pauses, stares, and wonders what he really experienced that night. In this he is no different from any of us, who fail to capture the truth in that mirror in which time is constantly dissolving certainty. The composer continues to note with puzzled affection the disappearance of all his sopranos, the transparency of all his many sincere disguises, as we may, thinking of our own.)

Yet when she sings for a moment, in that gilt drawing room, crammed with eternal projections, Sybil is Queen of the Night. "Lower to upper G," notes Massenet, "three octaves—splendid, and what a fine control. Also, she has fire and intelligence. Just look at the eyes! What promise for the stage. I'm convinced."

The next day he decides she is just right for the new part of Manon, or Esclarmonde, or Cendrillon, and starts to work on the score with a tremendously renewed intensity. A few months later, they are vacationing together in Switzerland.

They stay at the Grand Hôtel de Vevey—Massenet, Sybil, and her mother, who is going blind. The weather is crystalline, the mountains reassuringly theatrical. Massenet writes feverishly and fills up pages of his diaries with large-scrawled script, out of which the letter S rises obsessively, an emphatic treble clef for his song of passion. Meanwhile, there is much salon music, tutoring, many handkerchiefs, trembling hands, sighs, dreams, and finally, a seduction achieved with the appropriate complicity of both mother and daughter, the former blindfolded, the latter with her eyes closed. Yet the composer once again confronts that always familiar, ever strange dark gulf in which something nearly known continues to escape him. Soon after, the soprano begins to have doubts about her ability, decides to give up the part altogether and is reconciled to her duty only at the expense of many scenes. So the vacation continues, and the composing, while Massenet's wife Ninon and their daughter spend the summer elsewhere.

Ninon, of course, doesn't really count, though he has been careful through the years with his swooning over the ladies, and doesn't carry things far enough to drive her to desperate measures. Some inner genius has enabled him to calculate how much she will put up with to a very precise degree, and he always goes as far as he can for his pleasure, but not far enough to create the inconvenience of a major falling out with her. Of course, he has been from the beginning a true Romantic, ever requiring some particular embodiment of the muse to be at hand before he can edge himself into real creativity. Perhaps he was innoculated into this fevered rhythm of existence when he won the *Prix de Rome*, and spent some marvelous time in Italy, visiting the salon of none other than the great Liszt himself.

Massenet could never forget one of those nights in January in that city when he and some of his friends had gone for a stroll, and stumbled, quite by accident, into what seemed to be a vast ruined basilica, whose lurching arcades and coffered vaults teetered crazily against the murky sky. Stumbling forward, perhaps a little drunk, he saw, just above his unsteady line of sight, the spectre of a huge cross shining dimly from the darkness. He looked up at an infinity of blank sky, and peering around him, realized for the first time that he was completely encircled by colossal walls. His friends had meanwhile disappeared, and the immense and terrifying silence was disturbed only by his footsteps as he hurried past great fallen lumps of statues, and ancient cracked blocks of stone resembling ice in which even the faintest gleam of light had been snuffed out. But whichever way he turned he seemed to find himself back in the centre of the impossible maze. A clock chimed in the distance, and at that moment, the lurid, vulgar clang of Liszt's *Todentanz* rang in the young man's ears. Terrified, he lay down on some half-dilapidated steps, put his hands over his ears, and crouched there in stiff terror, until he finally went to sleep.

Dawn came, chilly but releasing. The sharp winter light pointed his way out of the Colosseum, that magnificent ruin which for one night the composer had shared with the cats of Rome.

That very day he met his future, present and eternal wife, Constance de Sainte-Marie, who is called Ninon. It was fine romantic idyll and Massenet gave her piano lessons, and pursued her for many months, until at last she yielded to his wishes and married him. The ceremony took place in a little church at Avon, one early October, and while the priest lectured the young couple and their guests on the Christian duties of marriage, a flock of sparrows whirled and danced and darted, chattering from outside the gleaming decorated windows, so that it was almost impossible to hear what he was saying.

Massenet managed to remain faithful to Ninon for a few years, before forming his first liaisons with the shopgirls of Paris and becoming insatiable. His manner during all of his lives is that of the "king-baby", the grown-up child sensualist who allows himself to be mothered by his wife and all women in exchange for a cooing placidity of manner that is unfailingly amiable. Leon Daudet compared him to a child or a lapdog, strutting and pawing his way through the drawing rooms with an insatiable eye for the ladies, always expecting to be petted for every incidental display of chivalry, helplessness, or musical talent. Then, finally, when from time to time he achieved his goal, and found himself in the arms of this or that ideal women of the moment he was surprised. Having convinced himself that he really cared about her, he found it difficult to understand why at the climax of sexual pleasure, he seemed to look into a blind, dark gulf, how at the supposedly perfect moment of this liaison or that, there was nothing personal, and whatever lady it was would vanish in a storm of bliss that seemed to obliterate her personality altogether, so that those qualities that had drawn him into the intimacy were never farther away than when the intimacy was complete. Snared by the fine silk sheets of those Parisian and Swiss hotels, a succession of female bodies became launching platforms which carried him into the cold, fiery regions of ultimate space, where he spun on a wheel of pleasure, always circling around a face that the final climax obliterated forever.

In this incarnation of his story, one of the many times he has watched the première of *Manon*, he begins to be very pleased with himself, astonished that anyone should have such a talent as he, suddenly listening to his music as a delighted stranger might. (But he fails to notice in the distance, outside around the countryside of Fontainebleau, the first stirrings of thunder, the hints of an approaching storm.)

The curtain goes up. The composer adjusts his set. It is a terrifying and beautiful moment, unfolding all those melodies by now so familiar to him that he can hardly bear to listen to them. He winces, but the thing is moving now, unstoppable, a headlong river of sound that he fears may suddenly trickle away under the stony resistance of an audience that in the end will dissolve in laughter and mockery.

But no; for now at least there is respectful silence; the orchestra plays together; Danbé, the conductor, seems to have things in hand. Massenet sits back, a little more relaxed, sipping his wine, watching the inn courtyard materialize before him—but what is Collin scowling about? Bretigny has nothing to scowl about at this point! The composer makes the first of many mental notes; tomorrow there will have to be corrections, adjustments. (But he fails to notice that the storm around the house has grown powerful; he fails to notice the staccato lightning, the shudders of thunder.)

Ninon has put down her knitting and has gone in search of the maid. In a minute they will be making their rounds, to be sure all the shutters are closed. In a minute they will come into the room where Massenet still stis oblivious, enthralled by the arrival of the coach carrying Manon.

Sybil steps out of the coach, wearing that perfect look of youth and innocence that he had coaxed from her for months. Soon, as the composer well knows, it will be transformed into an expression of longing for the great lyric life of passion and those brilliant cosmopolitan scenes. The catalyst will be the unfortunate Des Grieux, who will take advantage of Guillot's available carriage to rush Manon off to Paris, where their tragic story can begin to unfold. As he watches the familiar features of his beloved express the fresh nuance of every moment, and sees the intimately known body move lightly in its sheath of plain gray wool, Massenet is once again astonished at the ability of his protégé to assume a role. So powerful is the unity she has established with the character of Manon that she seems now almost to have become another person. If it were not for the voice, that divine, incomparable voice. . .

But suddenly the unity, the heavenly perfection of the rapport is broken. Ninon and the maid burst into the room, with jarring cries about the storm, the thunder. Startled, Massenet begins to struggle to his feet. All at once the lights go out everywhere.

"Damn!" cries the composer, knocking over the decanter, and blinking helplessly at the lumpish and unyielding darkness. The power supply has been cut off, and unless it returns, he will see no more of his precious *Manon* that evening.

It does not return. Massenet, frustrated beyond measure, prowls about nervously, maintaining an outward calm and the usual polish of his manner, but inwardly raging. Soon, having settled Ninon down and made inquiries about the cause of the disconnection, he comes to the conclusion that he must go at once to Paris. There is little chance power will be restored that night, but the storm has passed and the house seems to have been spared fire or accident. If he takes a fast transport vehicle he will just make it to the Opéra in time to receive the plaudits of the audience, which he is now inwardly sure must love his new work. But what a provoking situation nonetheless! To miss the greatest performance of his dear friend in a role that he had fashioned with the very tissues of his heart! It was unkind, the unkindest thing fate had so far afflicted him with!

The trip to Paris that night occurred without incident, but with much soul-searching by the composer as he sat in the privacy of his special compartment. Already he had some ideas for a new opera, for several new operas. It would only be a question of choosing the one that would do full justice both to his own talent, and to the wonderful voice of his incomparable Sybil. And from time to time, on that trip, as the lights flickered around him, and the night sky stretched away before his glance like the grand stage setting it could often be, the composer allowed himself to imagine what precise point his *Manon* had reached. Would they now be listening entranced to the dainty orchestral minuet that opens the third act? Would Des Grieux be singing mournfully of the haunting memory of his beloved: "*Ah! fuyez, douce image, à mon âme trop chère*". Surely *that* moment would wake up that filthy fat bourgeois in the fifth row, who by this time was drooling and fantasizing over his own shabby embodiment of the composer's beautiful heroine. 'Ah, Manon, they must all love you by now; they must love you even as I love you, as I have always loved you', sighed the distracted composer, shaken more than he could say by the night's strange events, and due to be shaken even further, a fact he actually intuited even then, through many dimensions of time, in the experience of so many varying scenarios of his life.

Once in the Opéra, released from the secret unpredictable life of the streets, Massenet was at home. He knew everyone, and nodded confidently to porters, stage hands, third assistant directors, costume ladies, and extras, convinced by the specific nuances of their startled surprise that the opera was over, that it was a success, but that he had much to hear about in the way of misadventures.

Danbé, he feared, has been responsible for a few blunders, or the lighting had failed at some point—some minor catastrophe that would be nothing in the triumph of the evening. For a triumph he knew it must be, as he penetrated deeper into the arcane private regions of the opera, and everyone who recognized him called out respectful congratulations, or stopped actually to bow and clap their hands in enthusiastic tribute. Before long the composer was virtually surrounded by a host of grateful and excited well-wishers, including a few distinguished patrons of the arts whom he recognized, and to whom he addressed a brief but far from perfunctory bow of thanks. He did not stop, however, but went on in search of Sybil, in search of Danbé, in search of Talazac, who he was sure had made a superb Des Grieux.

At last, turning down the corridor that led him to the very holy of holies, the dressing room area itself, by this time caught up in an excitement that he felt reflected upon him from all sides, the composer walked straight into several principals from the opera, still half in costume, led along by the ebullient Danbé.

"A success, master, a wonderful success," the conductor beamed, hardly able to contain himself, and almost taking the liberty of pounding the dignified composer on the back.

The cast crowded around, offering congratulations, and one of them, incredibly, was dressed in the prison rags of the fifth act, the rags Manon herself wears as she dies in the arms of Des Grieux at last. A muscial phrase shot all at once through the startled composer's brain: "Soon our happiness of old will come again". The whole pathos of the dying scene assaulted him, and combined with the unusual emotions of the night, nearly started a quite uncharacteristic fit of weeping.

But who was this dressed up as Manon? It was not Sybil, not his beloved Sybil, but Marie Heilbronn, whom he recognized at once, a beautiful Parisian soprano, noted for her fine acting and her scandalous life off-stage.

All at once Marie seized the arm of the startled composer, and bursting into tears confessed. "It's the story of my life. . . my own life!"

"She was exquisite, master, exquisite, " Danbé assured the dumbfounded Massenet. "The whole audience wept at the end."

Massenet raised his arm weakly, blinking at the strange, half-painted faced that surrounded him, unreal faces made harsh by the glare of lights from dim corners.

"But. . . Sybil. Madame Sanderson," the composer could barely get the words out. "She was. . .taken sick?"

"Unfortunately she couldn't sing at all tonight," Danbé was patiently explaining. "An accident at the last minute. She sprained her ankle. You didn't know?"

The composer detected a sudden tension around him, as if something vital were being concealed. But Danbé, seeming to sense Massenet's confusion and suspicion, hastened to reassure him:

"Of course, Madame Sanderson would have been superb, master. But think, such a substitute at the last minute! It's a triumph!"

The composer looks into the eyes of Marie Heilbronn. He has seen her many times but now he feels himself drawn to her as never before. She stands there, soft even in the unsparing glare of light that assaults them. Massenet thinks of how perfect she had been as he watched her from Avon, mistaking her for Sybil. He must go to Sybil now. But Manon is here.

Massenet bends to kiss the soprano's hand. It is a tribute to the real Manon, whoever she is. But already the composer has ceased to think of his opera, that perfect opera, already, under the influence of the evening's events, a new inspiration is awakening. For this beautiful woman who has saved his opera he will write the perfect, the incomparable role. This time, of all times, he feels himself on the track of some great wordless truth, capable of almost any depth of profound communication through the music that is beginning to stir in him.

Massenet turns with a light step, trying to call to mind Marie Heilbronn's address and the name of her most recent lover. Surely this time there would be no darkness, no blackout at the heart of the storm.

The Borges Transfer

When I first discovered the works of Jorge Luis Borges, my wife and I were running out the lease of a tiny apartment, convenient to the university where I was giving a series of lectures in the later developments of the theory of Socialist Realism. A few years before we had bought a house in the country, and enjoyed a spacious isolation and the complex pleasures of the simple life, but things soured, and our marriage nearly came apart. I was too wrapped up in my research, my wife complained, too monklike in my intellectual discipline; she wanted me to throw myself into a concrete world of gardening and mowing. There was a comical clash of equally absurd extremes, the humour of which occurred to us only later when we got back together after a short period of separation.

I at any rate realized then that even our break-up had been marked by that self-indulgent romanticism seemingly indispensable to our relationship. We had deceived ourselves in thinking that parting would be easy, and had tried to bedazzle ourselves with other relationships, which turned out to be only fleeting and superficial, though we found it necessary to play them up in our minds. Naturally, after such outbursts a period of recovery and truce was essential. It was beginning to be clear that almost nothing could free us from our bonds of mutual dependence, but clearly, we needed a rest.

The upshot was that after getting back together we moved into the city, storing most of our possessions, and occupying ourselves with a great deal of new work. We spent about ten months in the apartment (which my wife decorated with her usual ingenuity and imagination) but finally we decided to move out. In spite of the fact that the premises and location were nothing special, one potential renter after another appeared and was so impressed by our decor that we had many offers to take up the lease. I think these came from people who were charmed by those inimitable touches of my wife's decorating hand, which are too numerous and complex to mention, though I can give you a hint by referring to a lovely antique golden birdcage, out of which she had contrived to grow the most sinuously elegant and mysteriously twining ivy.

Borges, you know, is the famous South American writer, who fashions those elegant brief fables that affirm the reality of art over life. To Borges, as I learned soon after, nothing is real but the imagination: what we imagine becomes the truth in the most literal and sometimes ironic sense, as when a set of complex mathematical equations are simplified in a bomb. This writer had been recommended to my wife by one of her lovers, I think, during our separation, and in normal circumstances, this might have been enough to put me off, but under the tense conditions of our marital truce, it made reading him almost more piquant.

In a little while I had devoured almost everything available of the great Argentine, and while my wife continued to read almost nothing but murder mysteries, I had learned to appreciate touches like that in his story "Tlön, Uqbar, Orbis Tertius" in which a country is created that exists only so long as it is imagined. In this story, doorways and amphitheatres disappear when there is no one to think about them. Was Borges really a philosophical idealist; or was he subtly hinting at the existence of worlds that remain invisible because no one has yet imagined them for us? Did this mean that our familiar world too might become invisible, when imagination failed to renew our intimate connections with it?

Now at the time I was being led to consider these questions, one of the potential renters of our tiny apartment signed a lease, and we were free to move elsewhere. With a certain enthusiasm we decided to pursue our old preference for large houses with complex floor plans and with extra space that seemed to serve no earthly use. We moved only a dozen blocks away, but to a house many times the size of our apartment. I remember we packed our things for the movers and stopped, quite exhausted, at a local restaurant, while, in a mood of intimate, relaxed good-will, I explained to my wife the plot of one of Borges' most famous tales, which is called "The Library of Babel". In this story, the writer conceives of the whole universe as a vast library, and imagines many strange touches, such as people wandering endlessly throughout it, never able to master all of the texts, and sometimes disappearing after years of searching for even a single book that, among all those millions, might be identical with one other.

That night my wife and I slept in our newly rented house for the first time. We had made the arrangements with an old Italian woman, whose ad we had found in a local paper that ceased publication soon after. It seemed incredibly fortuitous. Finding decent housing in that particular area of town was always a difficult prospect yet we had chanced on a huge house at a very reasonable rent, in a remarkably short time.

True, there were problems with the place. It must have previously been occupied by extremely untidy hippie students, for it was very dirty and unkempt, and furthermore always seemed somewhat dark, no matter how we arranged the lighting. It was also vast. On the first night we slept on the third floor, listening to the great spaces of perhaps twenty (or was it thirty?) rooms reverberating around us with sharp but meaningless sounds. Lying there on a mattress on the floor, I was sorry I had not picked up that plate from downstairs, which seemed to have sat on a dusty window ledge for centuries, its cargo of chicken bones picked over more than once by mice or rats. I was also very sorry that my wife's golden birdcage with its trailing ivy had been damaged amid our upheaval. I had last seen it (in which room I forgot), the ivy drooping and faltering in the dull yellow light of that hectic evening, and I thought of it, just as I finally drifted vaguely into a kind of lazy, half-disturbed sleep.

The next morning, when I woke up, I noticed with some surprise that my wife was already up and gone. Usually, I had to wake her, to send her off to the government office in which she worked—she was a heavy sleeper. But now, the hollow groans and odd reverberations of the old house told me that I was alone in all of its creaking spaces. I was at first somewhat nonplussed, but soon recovered my equanimity, and picked up yet another volume of Borges, to while away the time, before I would have to do some work on my lectures. It was then that I read his essay "A New Refutation of Time", in which he seems to argue from the extreme position of the philosophical idealist: time is an illusion; we live only in the present; matter *per se* is an absurdity. Mind is the endlessly creative medium, and all literature becomes, for those who care to practice it, an act of identification. Thus, the fervent reader of Shakespeare *becomes* Shakespeare, the avid reader of Dante *is* Dante. And even these great names become almost insignificant in the still greater over-world which is the language system itself, every possible story repeated forever, with endless variations, across the distances of time, to make up a universe of discourse magnificent and terrifying

65

as the galaxies. . .

Was it really days later when I next saw my wife? The strange shadows of the house gave everything a dreamlike air and made all such conclusions uncertain. We sat silently, with almost nothing to say to each other. I had no inclination to tell her any more about Borges. I was not surprised when she wandered away upstairs without even saying good night

On another such evening, when she had seemingly gone to bed I decided that I wanted to explore the whole labyrinthian reality of the house. I took a flashlight with me, and began to wander through it, probing about the damp, fetid basement, where much of our luggage from the country had been piled for later sorting and unpacking. There was a curious quality I noticed here, which went on striking me as I attempted to make my way through the whole house. In every room, something specific would catch my eye, or intrigue me, so that I would almost forget the purpose of my tour, and stay there, for hours it seemed, wrapped up in aimless reveries.

These excursions went on night after night and on one of them I remember that I found a strange old book lying in a corner of the basement, thick with dust. It was half-hidden underneath a small box of frankincense and myrrh I had brought back from Arabia many years before. When I picked it up and started to look at it, however, the book seemed to fly out of my hands: it was a single long page folded up like a fan and set between two wooden boards. When you opened it upward from left to right, seemingly the wrong way, you could see quaint modern paintings representing certain Chinese sages and scholars, accompanied by sayings from their works. If you tried to open it in the usual way, however, turning the cover upward from right to left, you found a book with pages that were utterly blank. I couldn't remember ever buying this book, and was sure I had never seen it before. Either it was a recent acquisition of my wife, which she had forgotten to mention to me, or else it had been left behind by some earlier unknown tenant.

I must have sat for hours over this book, setting it up on a table like a child's house of cards, turning the pages in both directions, studying the curious detail of the drawings: the enigmatic smiles of the sages, the landscapes of trees and flowers receding into the distance. And soon certain of the phrases and sayings began to haunt my mind, mixing themselves up with the sentences of some Borges story or essay, so that as I walked slowly up and down the corridors, I seemed to hear a blur of secret mixed accents, cautioning me about illusions, about the chasms and distances between any single word and the next. . .

That was a long time ago, I think. I must bravely tell you the truth, which I know you have been expecting, and will accept, that I have not recently, in all my wanderings and searchings through this vastly complex labyrinth of rooms, met my wife. The house, it seems, is endless, as I discover anew each day, or hour, or minute, of my inspection. Floor after floor unfolds, bearing a slight resemblance to something I well remember, but which remains utterly alien. I have ambled now, possibly for ages, up and down those narrow stairs, sleeping on an odd mattress I chanced to find in some half-disordered corner, my ears attentive for the least sound of an approaching familiar voice, but always disappointed, for all I hear seems to be the echo of my own footsteps, or the amplified energies of my own breathing, which grows more and more distinct in the absolute silence around me. Just once, I wandered into a long dark corridor, indistinguishable from all the rest, on a floor I can't really remember, and I thought I saw, in the faint daylight, a clear girlish face peering at me anxiously from behind a half-open door. I moved closer at once, my heart beating rather wildly (I couldn't say why), but the girl had vanished. Perhaps I will meet her again, if she really lives here, or perhaps she is someone who dropped in by mistake, and is gone now though her face will register with me forever, like a flash of white alabaster beneath a dusty half-parted curtain. Perhaps, (who knows?) I mistook her completely, and it was my wife looking for me in these endless spaces, through all these infinitely gloomy rooms, even as I continue to look for her, trying to remember, minute by minute, what it was I wanted to say to her, as a last, most important communication from the silence of my own heart.

But all I can be sure of as I sit here, in this unfamiliar room, reading yet one more story of the master Borges, is that the last faint twirls of ivy have climbed back into the golden birdcage, and seem locked up forever in the dull light shining from one corner of this house which has finally become the whole universe for me.

Tourists from Algol

O ld Bob McClaren, on his way over to Harper's place with a big load of hay, was the first to notice that something was up at the newly laid-out river camp.

McClaren's tractor, a peeled red puffing monster, stalled unexpectedly at the top of a rise on the fifth concession, and the farmer had to get out quickly and block the wheels, holding the fat packed wagons in tow while he fumbled in his tool kit for the small wrench that just might do the trick.

It was a lovely day in July, typical of the season in that northern part of the province, the air a clear bouquet of the finest, the nights scrawled over with innumerable flashing stars. It's true the old folks swore the pollution was increasing something terrible, and everywhere south of the border the crisis continued — most of the Great Lakes finished now — but up north life went on pretty much as usual, nobody asked any questions, and the rare day of low sky and sulfuric smog prodded few to more than an occasional complaint, exchanged on the steps of the bank, or halfway through an especially dull night at the bowling alley.

Mostly, for the farmers in those parts, things seemed never to change — the prices grain and meat fetched were a scandal, expenses far too high, and interest rates so bad it was a wonder anyone could make an honest living anymore.

Around Easton's Corners nobody paid much attention either when the outsiders, foreigners it seemed, began buying up the best river land. They started by picking up all of Ronnie Wilson's pasture for a song after Ronnie died suddenly and Thelma was short of cash. Then, not long after, a big black air-conditioned Cadillac turned up at Stanski's place and a fellow wearing a headdress like a sheikh's got out. Joy Stanski claimed later that the chickens stopped laying that moment, but naturally that was her sense of humour. A couple of hours in the kitchen, a few follow-ups by telephone and the Stanskis had decided to get themselves a pollution free condominium in Miami — that's how good the offer must have been. It caused a bit of a stir and some talk at the post office, especially when word got around that the Bank had let go of its river land and that Domtar itself had cancelled plans to start a tree-fuel farm west of the fifth concession.

After that there was a bit of a hiatus. Crazy foreigners couldn't be expected to do the predictable thing, so nobody was very surprised when nothing happened for nearly a year. But then, prompt as if somebody's schedule was working, on the first of June, on a bright clear day when the fields had dried out after the spring rains, a whole army of earth movers, backhoes, stone crushers and trucks turned up on the nearby county road and rolled on down into the bought-out territory.

Before you could turn around, the whole place — it must have been nearly a thousand acres — was being fenced off and wired, wood and stone hauled every which way and some particularly oversize trucks bringing in load after load of bright shiny metal, plastic domes and coils of wire in quantities almost nobody had ever seen up to that day. And so the real construction work began, fast and furious.

It wasn't long either before the reeve and the town council were getting complaint after complaint about the noise, the state of the roads and the habits of the workers dragged in from the nearest big city. They had to explain that there really wasn't a darned thing they could do about it, nobody was violating any laws as far as they could see — it was just development, progress as folks used to say. As for dealing directly with the company, whatever it was, there didn't seem to be anybody to complain to. All the local bosses and foremen, and even the project manager were O.K. fellows, but they explained that they'd been hired from somewhere else, and that they were just carrying out contracts for somebody else. They had no idea who was responsible for the operation, other than that it was a private firm with branches all over, and with enough money to remake the moon if that was what they had a mind to do.

Then the school principal had a bright idea and decided to complain officially to the province. At first the response seemed only polite, but before long another of those air-conditioned Cadillacs arrived unexpectedly, and the town council was called into emergency session. This time it was *two* fellows dressed like sheikhs, and one in a dark business suit, who wore sunglasses which didn't come off once during the visit.

After a full day of parleying, word began to get around about the deal that'd been made. It seems the company was assuming full responsibility for the upkeep of the township roads, that two hundred jobs a year would be guaranteed for local folks as long as the operation went on, and that there would be a new centre, stocked with the best communications and emergency equipment, a place you could call with almost any kind of problem at any hour of the day or night, and expect help, and all for free at that.

This caused a lot of excitement, and kept the town council in office unopposed for the next three elections, but the most interesting thing, to some at least, was the rumour about what exactly was planned for the company development site. It seems that during one of the meetings old Gordon McKay had put it point blank to the fellow with sunglasses — that everyone would react a whole lot better if they actually knew what the company had in mind for the area. It would give folks something to chew on, as Gordon explained it, and make them feel part of things. Well, the fellow with the sunglasses was astounded, or pretended to be, that everyone didn't know already. "There's no secret about it," he reassured them, while the two sheikh fellows nodded and smiled, "we represent the Algol Tourist Development Corporation, and what we're putting up here at Easton's Corners is one of the world's most modern and exciting tourist park facilities." And then, just as the council members were all relaxing and nodding approval, he added something that a few picked up on later, and made something of. "Of course, there's one thing about this kind of facility that we insist on — it guarantees privacy to all guests, absolute and complete privacy to enjoy themselves in the ways they're most used to, consonant of course with the policy of the company and with universally established tourist practices."

So that was that, the negotiators went away, and the building continued for a while, as everyone digested what had happened and began to enjoy some of the benefits of the new arrangements. Then activity down at the river site seemed to stop, most of the city workers took off, and things were at a standstill until that day in July when Bob McClaren's tractor broke down (hopelessly, despite his handiness) and he had to walk to the nearest farm to call the emergency service the company had set up.

As McClaren trudged along the freshly paved concession road, he was able to get a good look down at the river camp, and noticed that something was definitely happening down there.

First of all, this was the only place in the whole area which overlooked much of the site. Not that you could see everything inside now that they had put up those large prefab walls everywhere, but the view was still impressive. McClaren peered down in amazement at acre upon acre of domes and spires, at structures like giant metallic mushrooms, at steel silos and gleaming switchbacks. There were antennae too, sprouting here and there among a profusion of oddly angled opaque barriers, and in the centre, or what seemed like the centre of everything, five mysterious glowing discs of light, which were even now pulsing and swelling in the clear July sunlight.

As McClaren continued to stare in amazement at this fantastic array of shapes, he noticed that some structures had been extended actually over the river, so that at one point the stream disappeared under a series of pointed triangular buildings on whose highly polished steel surface the farmer could see the reflected ghosts of clouds. Close to this spot was perhaps the most amazing sight of all, and when McClaren took it in, he actually swept off his tattered grimy old cap, put his hands on his hips, and just stood there shaking his head.

For some reason, between the pyramids by the river and a large clear green empty space that might have been a landing strip, the developers had placed what could only be a refurbished and toned-up but otherwise exact model of Mel Stanski's white clapboard farmhouse, barns and silo. McClaren could even fancy he saw Stanski's famous herd of Black Angus feeding there behind an old snake fence that looked like it had been built by somebody's grandfather. At that he simply gasped. But even that wasn't the final surprise.

While he was reflecting that amid all this profusion of strange and familiar buildings, there was no sign of any human activity, no sight of any guests or attendants, just machinery, his attention was attracted by the low distant humming of a powerful engine he took at first to be an airplane's. Over near Abbotsford, of course, a mere thirty miles away, there was a good-sized airport, but what now appeared, dancing up from the southern horizon like a bright speck of fire, was the strangest aircraft he had ever seen. As it raced closer at a great speed, and hovered finally a few miles away as if waiting for instructions, he could make out the shape very clearly: it was a large gleaming metallic craft, ringed with a double tier of bright portholes, a strange domed airship, simple and bright as a Christmas ornament, the first flying saucer that had ever been seen in the vicinity of Easton's Corners by a sober observer in broad daylight.

"Well, this sure *is* news!" McClaren said out loud to himself and wished he had some way of getting immediately to Maitland's store to talk it over. Of course by the time he got there everybody would have either seen or heard about the strange arrival, for arrival it most certainly was. As McClaren watched, the craft seemed to orientate itself there in the blinding blue sky, and then, without any further hesitation, it settled down for a perfect landing on the broad cleared space in the enclosure, right next to Stanski's farm.

At this point McClaren certainly held his breath. There was just no telling who or what was going to come out of that thing, and he sort of expected the worst. As a matter of fact, as far as he could tell, no one got out — the airship just took off again, and with a speed he wouldn't have believed unless he had seen it with his own eyes, it made off in the direction of Abbotsford.

Well, that was the beginning of the tourist invasion of Easton's Corners, because after that the strange ships began a regular schedule of runs, both summer and winter, into the little community. Just about once a week they appeared, always the same domed vehicles coming up from the south (from where, no one knew), hovering a moment like high peering hawks, and then landing, presumably in the very place Bob McClaren had seen them touch down. As a matter of fact it was impossible to know exactly where they landed, and more importantly, who or what came off, because when word got around about McClaren's point of vantage it was quickly delcared off limits to the locals, under threat of cancellation of the whole project. Barriers were put up and some townsfolk were recruited to stand guard.

At the same time the tourist park became a very lively place, and the centre of absolutely everyone's attention, at least at first. When the airships started coming in, people could talk about nothing else. At the scheduled times, they stood in little groups outside of Maitland's store or the post office and exchanged opinions about just who the tourists were, where they came from, and what in the name of heaven they'd be doing with themselves at Easton's Corners. It was all the more frustrating, then, all the more provoking, when it became evident that nothing was known about these visitors, that they were not going to reveal themselves, that even so much as a glimpse of them was to be denied the inquisitive townsfolk.

The tourist park was lively enough, though, that was clear. Every night until all hours it was a veritable circus of lights, a Matto Grosso of strange noises. Whistles and bells, eerie wails, the bleating and howling of unknown voices, together with something that to many of the townsfolk sounded very much like an amplified moo, came racketing out of there, and certainly complaints might have been expected had not the heritage fund been quickly doubled, so that there was promise of an easy retirement for many. The lights were not so bothersome, and some even got to enjoy them and sat outside in the summer for the show.

Quite soon after the first visitors came to the park the bus tours started. These were not any ordinary jaunts with eager tourists craning necks at the windows, however. The big park gates simply opened one morning and out rolled the oddest machine, a giant silver thing on wheels with the quietest engine anyone had ever heard, with big portholes that folks ran to gape at, only to find they were polished metal and could be seen through, presumably, only from the other side. This machine swung blithely around town, and indeed the whole area, as if the driver owned the place and sometimes it would stop in the strangest corners, while at the portholes the curious saw or imagined the tiniest little flashes of green light, and a loudspeaker poured out a slithery-voiced palaver of high-pitched meaningless sounds. That was extremely provoking, and quite soon people learned to ignore these buses out of pride, pretending they had much better things to do than to take part in such a one-sided contact with such curiously intruding and uppity foreigners.

As a matter of fact, at first at least, there was quite a bit to do. A little factory was established and certain foods were manufactured, to be sold or otherwise provided to the tourists. The products of this factory did seem rather strange. Chemicals that no one really could figure out were flown in and assembled on the spot into brightly coloured jellies, crunchy little morsels that resembled candy bars, and drinks that were highly carbonated but so sweet that no one could swallow more than a teaspoonful without wincing. Vast quantities of such stuff were carried to the park in small delivery trucks. Like everything else coming from town, these goods were handed over to the park attendants, who were not locals and who never left the grounds, except for some particular business of the day.

At the same time, it became noticed that these attendants, who rode the buses with the tourists, would often jump out at certain points on the routes and make rather fabulous offers for any of various local products that happened to be available on the spot. Old wagons, farm implements of all kinds, the town's only barbershop pole, as well as a surprising number of backhouses were sold off in this manner. When word got around, some people actually began to pile their furniture and other items out on their porches in hope that one of the tourist buses would pass by and they could make a quick sale. After a while, when nearly eveything portable seemed to have gone, it was rumoured that some people had started to make a good living creating imitations of traditional products. They would create such imitations virtually overnight and then sell them to interested parties, who in turn would pass them off to the tourist buyers at greatly exaggerated prices.

At first these practices were denounced by some, but events soon gave them far more serious matters to complain of. It seems that the local food factories (there were three of them by this time) were not only producing the candied edibles and sweet-tasting drinks already mentioned, but also a clear white potent liquor that soon became the rage among the townsfolk, especially the younger set. There was almost no way, it seemed, to stop certain ingredients from being smuggled out of the factories (or maybe the managers had no interest in doing so) — at any rate, before long many of the younger people of the town were having wild parties celebating their conversion to "algolism", as one local wit named their addiction to this powerful brew. Drunkenness was certainly on the increase, and this meant more automobile accidents (a few resulting in terrible injuries) and in brawls in the streets at all hours. When representations about this continuing scandal were made to the town council, it was decided, not to ban the drink, but to increase the policing effort and to set up a curfew. Some of the youngsters, it seems, were from powerful local families, and any absolute prohibition was out of the question.

So the security forces came into being. Many of the local youngsters themselves (especially the ones who were interested in nothing else and were, in plain language, layabouts) were lured into this force by the high pay and the chance to wear uniforms and to carry weapons in public. (The nearest station of the provincial police was ten miles in the direction of Abbotsford and no one wanted to call on them and risk a reaction against the young people and possibly a setback in terms of the increasingly lucrative company spending). The security force therefore seemed the only alternative. It's true that oldtimers were shocked, and claimed this was a development that went right against the grain of everything the country stood for, but when it was pointed out to them that several among them had been beaten up by drunken youths during the past several months, they simply shook their heads and accepted the situation.

As if this wasn't bad enough there was the celebrated case of Reeve McIntyre. From the beginning he had led the movement of cooperation with the company, and had taken the lead in welcoming their representatives (mostly Americans and Arabs) who were always engaged in negotiating some point or other with the townsfolk. Over the years McIntryre seemed to prosper markedly as a result of his efforts, but then, since the whole town was similarly prospering, no one questioned the situation. It was only when the reeve failed to show up at three consecutive council meetings that people began to ask just where he was and why, if he had suddenly departed, he had left no word with anyone. A tight-mouthed old bachelor, he lived in a white frame house at the edge of town and kept very little company locally, preferrring to go to Abbotsford and even beyond for his entertainment. When no word of his whereabouts came, an investigation was made and it was discovered that several hundred thousand dollars was missing from the town's heritage fund. It was further discovered that during the previous several years McIntyre had transferred large sums of money to an external account he maintained in a Bahamian bank. The cry of protest was now extreme and a little group of rebels led by a schoolteacher suggested that all the operations of the company be fully investigated and that all the remaining council members make complete financial disclosures. The council promptly resigned *en masse*, but it was decided, out of a desire for good relations with the company, to keep everything as quiet as possible. The bare legal requirements would be fulfilled, but in order to ensure the approval of the Algol corporation, there would be no general investigation of anyone.

At this point it became clear to a few that the arrival of the company had not meant a straight line of improvement for Easton's Corners. What had once been a sleepy but well-functioning little community had now almost no working farms. Most of the locals had given up cultivating the land in favour of manufacturing treats for the tourist park; or else they spent their time turning out instant antiques. The young people had certainly stopped running off to the cities at age sixteen or so. That would have been foolish with so much free drink and easy employment available locally, but as it happened most of them grew bored with the life of the town and left anyway in their early twenties. There was constant talk, of course, about the great increase in local income — most of this, it seems, went into buying larger television sets and more expensive cars, and there were rumours that, even apart from the McIntyre swindle, there were flaws in the set-up of the heritage fund that might in the long run deprive many of their promised and long hoped-for rewards.

So the anger of some few grew at the company, and in fact a point was reached where Chartier, the local teacher who had previously wanted an investigation, circulated a petition denouncing the company and asking for a provincial inquiry. In the text he demanded that the Algol Corporation cease at once its role of faceless intruder and meet directly with the local people, that the corruption of local life stop, and that a reform program be introduced. Shortly after these demands were discussed at a council meeting, Chartier's house burned down and his wife and children barely escaped with their lives. There was no evidence of arson, but the teacher decided to move to one of the abandoned farms on the outskirts of town, and to take every precaution within the law.

The teacher's reference to the faceless owners once again raised the question of exactly what the tourist visitors looked like, and why they had chosen to set up in Easton's Corners in the first place. No one quite dared approach the company with the suggestion that access be allowed to the park, but the local manager (who was from New York) explained during a long session with the council that the company's interest in Easton's Corners was based on its high evaluation of the place as an authentic link with the great Canadian rural tradition, one that had vanished almost everywhere else in the country. The visitors came, he explained, because they had a great desire to experience this local culture in completely protected and private circumstances, and to enjoy their own customs with the least possible danger of disturbing the vital currents of the indigenous ways of life. This interesting (and indeed flattering) answer satisfied the whole council, though Chartier, who stormed out at one point, was heard to murmur something about a "monstrous illogicality."

Rumours continued to circulate, of course, about the exact nature and condition of the unseen guests, and many kinds of speculation occurred over the years. It was suggested that they might be black tourists from the new Africa kept hidden so as not to shock the local sensibilities. Or that they were mentally retarded adults from the States who were being flown in at the expense of some generous company charity. Or even that they were highly placed executives of various powerful companies who had come up to this isolated spot with girl friends for a little private orgying in an atmosphere free of pollution or of the elaborate climate-controlled environments Americans were by now used to. There were even weirder rumours, fed mostly by the unauthenticated story of some boy scouts who had been canoeing in the vicinity of the tourist park, and who had accidentally trespassed into one of the private channels of the river normally hidden from sight by the pyramidal enclosures. These boys, returning home in a rather hysterical state after abandoning their canoe and camping equipment, kept insisting that they had seen giant lizards, laughing and chattering and hugging each other in one of the brightly lit recesses under the central pyramid by the river. This was generally scoffed at and was put down to their watching too many science fiction movies. It wasn't the first time this kind of rumour had circulated, but then it was mainly among the younger folks, most of whom had seen such movies as *Star Wars* and its successors as many as twenty or thirty times.

What became known only to the very few, on the other hand, was that one night someone showed up, at an exceedingly late hour, at the farm now occupied by the Chartier family. Chartier, who had grown very nervous, greeted the visitor with a shotgun and refused to let him in until the man had emptied his pockets and agreed to sit across the table without making any sudden movement in the teacher's direction. The visitor, however, claimed to be talking to Chartier at the risk of his life anyway. He sat there, speaking both English and French fluently, but with a strong Spanish accent — a sallow little man with a dark drooping mustache. He was, he claimed, the contact man of a resistance movement in a well-known South American country which he named. While Chartier listened, the man outlined the manner in which his country had been colonized by outside forces, including the notorious Algol Corporation, which he claimed was a completely alien operation, out for maximum profit at any cost. He pointed out how in his country the local economy had seemed to prosper under the influx of foreign money, and how people had bent over backwards to accommodate the activities of the newcomers, including their tourism. Nonetheless, little by little, freedom had been lost, and the promised prosperity had never really come. It turned out that those who played the company game got rich while others lost ground, or failed to rise out of their misery. When protests occurred, the company turned to violence, with the full approval of the government in power. The only solution seemed to be to undertake full resistance including sabotage and guerilla actions against the intruders. It was important

78

as well that the various movements of resistance around the world establish contact, since the enemy operated on a global scale. He was now proposing that Chartier agree to become leader of the local movement.

Chartier was naturally astounded, and had many questions, after the first few moments of shocked silence with which he greeted this speech. Like most North Americans, he had never thought of politics in these terms at all, and violence was something very far away from his upbringing and education. All he could say to his visitor was that he would consider his words very seriously, but that he must have some time to think things over. The man disappeared, but standing at Chartier's door just before his departure, he made one final dramatic little speech. It was obviously quite sincere but it sounded a little exaggerated, perhaps due to the Spanish flavour of the man's delivery.

"There are those who will argue that even to question the right of the tourists to come is a politically subversive act," he declared. "Yet I predict that partisans living in the woods and subsisting on venison, rabbit and scraps of garden produce stolen from the visitors, will never doubt the integrity of the environment they inhabit and will gladly pay for this environment with their lives. They will take for granted that death itself has sanctified the evergreen forests, the lake-strewn lands of the north. Perhaps, however, this is only another form of deceit; perhaps death sanctifies nothing. Even so, the battle must be considered a righteous one. If you agree, join us."

Sometime after this incident, recounted by his wife only to their closest friends, Chartier disappeared. There was speculation that he had left out of fear. Some said he was going underground to lead the resistance. His wife protested bitterly that since she had had no word from him, he might have been abducted or even murdered by the company, and she tried to start an investigation. After some debate, the council decided to shelve the whole business for lack of concrete evidence.

In Easton's Corners meanwhile, life went on as usual, though day by day the traditional ways were left farther behind and new problems arose to bedevil the little community. If the situation didn't exactly add up to complete prosperity, it couldn't be said either that there was a lack of progress in certain areas. As for the visitors, no one ever really did see them, not for certain, and interest was only aroused again when it was rumoured that the Algol Corporation was pulling out its whole operation to relocate in a more unspoilt area of the north. There was quite an outcry then, and many representations from groups of every kind, but still, very few local folks had a bad word to say about the tourists themselves. The feeling was probably best summed up by old Bob McClaren, who had lived through the whole business, evaluated all the rumours for what they were worth, and decided that though the tourists might be a little shy, and the company a little greedy, taken all in all, they were regular folks and deserved the same fair shake as everyone else.